JUSTICE WITHOUT MERCY

A HARRY BAUER THRILLER

BLAKE BANNER

RIGHTHOUSE

PRAISE FOR HARRY BAUER

"Thor, Baldacci, Flynn, Hamburg. Get ready as Banner fits right in!"

AMAZON REVIEW

"Move over Jack Reacher there's a new guy taking over."

AMAZON REVIEW

"Great stuff. Exciting and fast paced. On par with Flynn & Thor."

AMAZON REVIEW

The characters and events portrayed in this ebook are fictitious. Any similarity to real persons, living or dead, is coincidental and not intended by the author.

ISBN-13: 978-1-63696-476-8

ISBN-10: 1-63696-476-1

Printed in the United States of America

www.righthouse.com

www.instagram.com/righthousebooks

www.facebook.com/righthousebooks

twitter.com/righthousebooks

HARRY BAUER THRILLER SERIES

Dead of Night (Book 1)
Dying Breath (Book 2)
The Einstaat Brief (Book 3)
Quantum Kill (Book 4)
Immortal Hate (Book 5)
The Silent Blade (Book 6)
LA: Wild Justice (Book 7)
Breath of Hell (Book 8)
Invisible Evil (Book 9)
The Shadow of Ukupacha (Book 10)
Sweet Razor Cut (Book 11)
Blood of the Innocent (Book 12)
Blood on Balthazar (Book 13)
Simple Kill (Book 14)
Riding The Devil (Book 15)
The Unavenged (Book 16)
The Devil's Vengeance (Book 17)
Bloody Retribution (Book 18)
Rogue Kill (Book 19)
Blood for Blood (Book 20)

The Cell (Book 21)
Time to Die (Book 22)
The Reaper of Zion (Book 23)
Justice Without Mercy (Book 24)
Bad Blood (Book 25)

ONE

Can vengeance be any part of justice? There are plenty of people in this broken world who will tell you that if a guy breaks into your house and rapes, mutilates, and murders your daughter or your wife, you should engage in a meaningful dialogue with him, to discover what deep pain or sense of dispossession led him to do it—like his motivation makes what he did somehow OK.

And maybe you should even consider that what he did is actually your fault. For existing in the first place.

I am not a philosopher or a lawyer, but I know that justice is about balance, and so is vengeance. This a cruel world where in order simply to survive, we have to eat each other. Literally, not figuratively. In that kind of world, when your daughter or your wife has been raped, mutilated, and murdered, meaningful dialogue will not bring them back. But it will allow the bastard who killed them to believe he can do it again and do what the hell he likes and get away with it. Blowing his brains out will not bring them back either, but it will stop him doing it to anybody else, and it will let his pals know that hurting innocent people has consequences.

That is about the extent of my philosophy.

I had been thinking about that kind of stuff for a couple of months at my log cabin in Pinedale, Wyoming. I'd been sitting on my deck, taking a rest, looking at the Wind River Mountains across the plain, watching the mustang running half-wild in the fields below my house on the hill. Earlier, I'd been chopping wood for the long winter ahead, and while I did all those things, I had been telling myself it was time to accept the fact that little Miriam had gone from this world[1]. She had found her peace and was no longer a ghost who haunted me and drove me to revenge; and Dr. Claire Erickson was no longer the woman who was going to rescue me from my darkness[2].

I was a killer. Colonel Gordon of the IDF had called me *Mal'akh ha-Neqamah*, the angel of vengeance. And if I never killed another man again in what was left of my life, I would still always be nothing but a killer. It's what I am: an angel of death.

It was into this private, hermetic world that Brigadier Alexander 'Buddy' Byrd drove on the early afternoon of Monday, September 15th. I was sitting on the fence, watching the mustang and wondering which one I was going to take for my own, when I saw a silver Cherokee pull into the drive a quarter of a mile down the hill. It took its time grinding its way up the track and ground to a halt as I swung down from the fence. The driver's window was open, and as I approached, I saw it was the brigadier. He smiled.

"Got a drink for a weary traveler?"

---

1. See *Reaper of Zion*
2. See *The Devil's Revenge* and *Time to Die*

"No, but I have got a couple of drinks and a bison steak, if you're man enough."

He laughed, and I followed him up the drive and across the small wooden bridge over the creek in front of my house. There I climbed onto the deck that runs around my house and made for the fridge, while he parked his truck out back by the kitchen door. That was where I met him with a cold bottle of beer.

"Very welcome," he said and drained half of it on the doorstep. He dumped a leather Gladstone bag by the stairs and wiped his mouth on his sleeve. "You're pretty remote up here. Got somewhere I can crash for the night?"

I smiled. "Sure, you can sleep in the stable with the horses, as long as you don't snore. They're light sleepers." I moved over to the fridge and pulled out a couple of steaks. "I've got four bedrooms up those stairs. Mine's the one with a P226 hanging from the bedpost. Take your pick of the other three."

He drained the last of his beer, muttered something about being better off with the horses, and carried his bag upstairs.

Twenty minutes later, we were seated at the big hunk of polished redwood that served me as a table, and the brigadier paused in his eating to lean back and glance at me while he put his napkin to his mouth.

"Harry, we have a delicate matter to discuss."

"The colonel says I blew up too many things, and now you want me to take early retirement.[3]"

He chuckled. "Even Jane is coming to understand that you only blow things up when you absolutely have to. Which, I confess, seems to be most of the time. No, I don't want you to take early retirement. Neither does she, for that matter. Quite

---

3. See, e.g. *Immortal Hate* and *The Silent Blade*

the contrary, but I do want you to go a little beyond the usual Cobra brief."

I nodded down at the bison sirloin on my plate. "So is this a Cobra brief? Or is it a private enterprise?"

He sighed and examined his glass of Muga, like the answer to my question was in there somewhere.

"A bit of both. Let us say it starts as a private enterprise, and depending on the intelligence you gather, it might become a Cobra brief."

"OK."

"We have received reports which we need to confirm." He paused and gave what he'd just said some thought. "Who is we?" he said. "The answer to that is confidential, so let's say I. I want you to take not early retirement but a holiday. If on that holiday you can confirm that the reports we have are accurate, then the Cobra brief will become active."

"What are those reports?"

He nodded, like he agreed with the question. "You know that lithium is rare and extremely expensive."

I echoed his nod. "Sure."

"There are few places on Earth where it can be found, and its value to..." He paused and arched an eyebrow at me. "Its value to defense contractors is incalculable. The American war machine is the deadliest, most powerful machine this planet has seen in fifteen thousand years. But take away its electronic capabilities, and the entire military industrial *intelligence* complex of the Western world becomes very vulnerable indeed."

"So we are talking about mining."

He nodded rather ponderously. "Partly. We are talking about an *alleged* mining operation on a small island nobody has ever heard of."

I frowned. "OK, where is that?"

"St. Homer." He glanced at me. "That's with an H, like the Greek poet. The origin of the name may have been a joke originally because the native inhabitants back in the sixteenth century were the I-Takka tribe who spoke a dialect of Lokono. They called the island I-Takka, which in their dialect might mean stone or, as it is spelt, it could mean 'I go.' Nobody is left who speaks that dialect, so we shall never know. However, Itaca in Spanish, pronounced as in Greek ee-taca, refers to Ithaca, Odysseus' homeland. So St. Homer with an H might have been an erudite joke. Or it might refer to the seventh century bishop, St. Audomar, who was also known as St. Omer..."

He trailed off, having apparently lost his thread. I said, "We shall never know."

"Quite. We shall never know. However, the island, which is just seven miles long and three across at its widest point, lies some seventy miles off the Atlantic coast of South America, precisely between Guyana and Surinam. Both countries lay claim to it, but neither has been willing to make any kind of military move to take possession of it, lest it be perceived as provocative. The claims went to arbitration back in the late '70s. They were overseen by the United States, but that process seemed to stagnate round about the time Mr. Stanley Whittingham's work on the lithium battery got seriously underway at Exxon. Nobody since then has seemed terribly keen to kick-start it again, either."

"Is that odd?"

"Maybe. There are inhabitants on the island. There is a city hall, apparently, but it is pretty basic. There is no formal census of the population, as you'd imagine, but estimates put it at about two thousand people, probably more. They are a mix of Portuguese, Spanish, French, native Indians, and descendants of African slaves. As far as we can tell, there are three towns, one of which is a functioning port, Puerto Ste. Maria. There is a town hall—what you would call City Hall—in Es Arenal, the capital of the island. Nobody pays income tax, or any kind of tax for that matter, so there is a question mark over how the town hall is funded."

"What about law enforcement?"

"Apparently there is a sheriff, but one has to ask, if there are no taxes, who pays him and his deputies? Who pays for the office and the gas in their trucks?"

He took a deep breath. "And the key issue here is that there *might* be a mine somewhere on the island, producing lithium for interests within—"

"The military industrial intelligence complex. And that mine is paying for the administration of City Hall and, most important, law enforcement. I.e., they own the island and the people on it."

"Precisely."

I ate for a moment in silence, then asked, "Why is that a problem? Why might it concern Cobra? Even if we disapprove of some of their methods"—I gave a small shrug—"or even their existence, we are a part of the military industrial intelligence complex. We need them, and they need us."

"That's true, in the abstract. But all too often, that complex ends up perpetrating everything we exist to fight against."

"Crimes against humanity."

"There are pieces"—he shook his head, searching for accurate words—"elements such as minerals, chips, processors—thousands of different parts—that go into American and NATO armaments and defense technologies that were mined or made by abused and exploited people. It is an industry that by its very nature *must be* amoral. So it is very difficult to decide where to draw the line. What abuses and exploitations you are going to..." He paused and took a deep breath. He didn't like the words available to him. "I'm not going to say turn a blind eye to. We don't. We can't. We know what is happening in those mines and factories, but the price of taking action is too high. It would damage our defense industry and make us too vulnerable."

I nodded that I understood. "The extremes are clear. You can't execute a man for shouting at an employee or paying him a poor wage. You can't not execute a man who enslaves, rapes, tortures, and murders children, but as you narrow the gap, where do you draw the line? Where does it become unacceptable?"

"Precisely. What we do is accept and tolerate because our position as the most powerful military in the world necessarily depends on that industry."

He sipped his wine, and as he set down his glass, he produced a rueful smile.

"It's a funny thing, though. Even if it is hard sometimes to know what we will tolerate. When it comes down to it, we know exactly what we *won't* tolerate. Those things you listed: child slavery—any kind of slavery but especially child slavery—is intolerable. Rape and sexual abuse, torture and murder, are beyond what we can tolerate if we are to remain human. And *if* what we have been told is accurate, all of these things are going on at the mine."

He wiped his mouth with his napkin and dropped it on the table.

"I say that," he went on, "but we don't even know for sure that there is a mine."

"Satellite imagery?"

"There is something there, but exactly what it is is unclear. It seems there is some kind of electromagnetic field interfering with the satellite images."

I leaned back in my chair and crossed my arms. "But there must be bills of lading, contracts of sale, shipping documents, some kind of electronic or paper trail that indicates tons of lithium are being purchased—"

"That is very logical, and of course it's the first thing we looked at, but for a start, we are dealing with very obstructive, secretive defense contractors. These are departments and organizations that tell Congress to go to hell. In the second place, in many cases, this lithium winds up in places like Cabinda Itumbe or Mozambique, in Africa, or Malaysia and Singapore in Asia, or Buru, in Indonesia. In remote, deeply corrupt places like that, its origin becomes impossible to trace; and in the third place, as I mentioned earlier, I-Takka's jurisdiction is not so much not clear as non-existent. There is no legislature and therefore, technically, no law. And nobody is in a hurry to bring either into existence. So the laws governing shipping from the Port of Santa Maria are equally nonexistent. What leaves the Port of Santa Maria in those container ships is sometimes ambiguous to the point of absurdity. I have seen entries like 'mineral cargo' 'raw goods,' and even 'various.' So paper trails and electronic trails lead invariably down blind allies."

"So you need boots and eyes on the ground. What exactly do you want me to do?"

"As you can imagine, assuming there is any truth in the allegations, if Central Intelligence investigates, they will return having found no evidence at all because they serve the military industrial intelligence complex completely. They were virtually created by the same act of Congress.

"However, Cobra can't commission intelligence gathering.

That is well beyond its remit. So what I am asking you to do is totally unofficial. All I ask is that you go on holiday."

"They have infrastructure for that? Hotels, beach resorts...?"

"Oh, yes. They have hotels, bars, restaurants. It's not a place that is frequented much, so it's pretty basic, but if it turns out to be a false lead, you can at least have an enjoyable holiday on Cobra. We owe you a good rest."

"OK, I'll be happy to do that."

"I have a map of the island, documents, cash, all that stuff. But essentially you'll find the island has three large hills covered in dense pine forests on the far western extreme. As you head east and south toward Puerto Santa Maria, the island flattens out, and there are areas of gorse, moss, and bare rocks that form rocky cliffs jutting into the ocean. The center of the island, however, is made up of dense, fertile pine forest which thins out toward the east into what I can only describe as rolling downs. Beyond them is another area of hard, rocky cliffs that juts out into the sea with a lighthouse at the end. The intelligence we have indicates that this is the area where the mine is, on the North Faro Road."

"Hotels, car rentals..."

"All that information is in the file which I'll give you when you make the coffee and break out some of your excellent Irish single malt. I would like you to study it and decide how you want to approach it. After all, you are just going on holiday. You have nothing to hide, no hidden agenda..." He spread his hands.

I nodded. "Sure. Let's do it. I'll make the coffee."

TWO

We landed at Cheddi Jagan International Airport at nine a.m. local time. It was small enough to still be human. You could walk across the tarmac to the terminal building and deal with customs and passport control right there in the main hall, in full view of the plate glass windows and the country outside, without going through a single tunnel.

A guy from the British embassy with floppy, sandy hair was there. He shook hands warmly with a firm grip like he was really pleased to meet me.

"Mr. Bauer, I'm Andy, good to meet you, welcome to Guyana. We have a car outside..." He guided me toward the exit. "I'd offer you a lift to the port, but Buddy asked us to keep a low profile. However, we *do* have a few goodies for you in the boot. That's the trunk to you. Going to I-Takka, I understand. We've been keeping an eye on the place for a while."

"Have you got anyone over there?"

"Sadly, no. Our administration is in the hands of morons at the moment, I'm afraid. They think the way to make Britain great again is to cut all investment that brings a benefit or a yield and invest only in the black hole of social benefits for unqualified immigrants."

I laughed. "Hey, don't hold back on my account. Say what you really mean."

"Quite." He chuckled. "You know, make England—as opposed to Britain—great again, as an acronym, becomes MEGA. I think that's rather good, don't you? Here we are..."

I smiled as he opened the trunk of an old Bentley. "That's pretty good," I said. "It might even happen one day, when you stop hating yourselves."

He pulled out a Gladstone bag and set it at my feet.

"Quite. Mr. Bauer. I don't know what you're going to find on I-Takka. I *should* know, because it probably affects the balance of power on this planet, but our politicians are far too busy trying to get reelected and pursuing their own, sad little share of power instead of protecting our sacred Western values. Spain faced the same problem in 1936, and that resulted in a civil war that was the first ripple of the most devastating global war the world had ever seen." He smiled. "I am an historian, Mr. Bauer. History, like garlic, repeats itself. I hope I am wrong, but I fear we are about to see a very nasty belch, with the UK in the role of Spain."

By the time he'd finished, I was frowning hard. I wanted to ask him to explain, but he laughed and said, "Don't let me get on my hobby horse, Mr. Bauer. I am infamous for it."

He made for the driver's door but stopped and turned back. He pointed at the bag.

"Everything is there. On your way back, perhaps we could have a drink in town, and I'll drive you to the airport."

I nodded. "I'd like that."

He drove away, and I carried my two bags back to the

terminal. There I grabbed a cab and told the driver to take me to the port in Georgetown. It was a comparatively short distance, past low, attractive houses set by the river among abundant lush green palms and pine trees. All the way, the driver told me about how the people from Surinam were devious and cunning and could not be trusted. “If they don’t stab you comin’ in, they gonna stab you goin’ out!” he told me, then added that they were basically the same people as in Guyana. “We all brothers an’ sisters, right? Indians, the other Indians, Africans, Spanish, Europeans, British. Hey!” He threw his hands in the air, and ash sprayed from his cigarette. “Come on! They should understand that! Right?”

“Right.”

As we moved down the broad main street of the small city, past the sugar-brown water of the Demerara River, he asked me, “Where you goin’? You catchin’ a boat?”

“St. Homer?”

“I-Takka?” He let out a long, high-pitched hoot. “Maaan, I hope you got sea legs! You got three hours of uuuup and down, up and doooown!” He demonstrated with his hand going up and down over rolling waves, screamed laughter like a parrot, and pounded his steering wheel with the heel of his hand. “I-Takka, maaan. Tha’s belong to us, man. You know that? Tha’s Guyana. But Surinam, you know, they move in an’ took it. You was right to come through Guyana, man. Yeah.”

Georgetown is a chaotic, messy city that fails to be delightful because of it. It has beautiful, colonial architecture, colorful markets everywhere you could squeeze in a colorful market, and the people are as open and friendly as people could be, but the town, or as much of it as I saw, was just plain ugly and messy. Everywhere you look, what you see speaks of don’t give a damn.

The taxi dropped me outside the ferry terminal on Brickdam Street beside the massive, teaming Stabroek Market. The market stands on the docks at the mouth of the Demerara River, where it spills out into the Atlantic, and the whole area is a nervy, chaotic jumble of fruit, yams, kitsh clothes and jewelry, Black women in blazing robes and headdresses, the rich smells of coffee and spice, and a million shouting voices.

It took me a while, shouldering my way through the crowds, but eventually I found a wooden shack beside the quay. It had a sign over the door which, if you cleaned away the grime, would have read *Ferry Georgetown – I-Takka*. Inside there was a guy leaning his elbows on the counter and his face on his left hand. He looked so bored I found myself checking him for cobwebs.

"I need a passage to I-Takka. When's the next ferry?"

He took a deep breath, blinked his big black eyes, then shifted his gaze from the bright street outside to smile at me.

"Da's gonna be ten thousand five hun'red dollars, my friend. The St. Homer is departin' at eleven a.m. this mornin', sir."

I gave him the money, and he tore a ticket off a pad and handed it to me. Then he leaned forward, frowning, smiling, and shaking his head all at the same time.

"Maaan," he said, "is a *quiet* day. A *quiet* day. I think you gonna be alone on that boat."

The boat turned out to be on the far side of ancient. Probably from the early '60s, it was made of rusty steel that creaked and groaned and clattered when we went over the swollen, rolling waves. The guy had not been far wrong. I was pretty much alone on the boat, aside from a large woman with skin so black it was almost purple and robes and headdress so brilliant and colorful she seemed to vanish inside them. She had an old, battered brown suitcase and sad eyes. I wondered what her story was.

At the far end of the boat, sitting on the rear deck, there was a guy, tall and lanky, with a drinker's nose and grizzled gray hair that still had streaks of blond in it. He had his face plastered against the glass, and he was snoring the snore of the drunk.

It was about a mile and a half to the mouth of the river. As we rounded the sea wall, we sighted the Georgetown Marriott glistening and isolated in the morning sun, and shortly after that, the sea began to swell and the St. Homer started to rear and roll and corkscrew, groaning and creaking as the engine struggled and changed its pitch with every wave. A few miles after that, as the coastline began to fall away behind us, the wind rose and the swell grew higher, with some of the waves spitting salty spray into the air, and now and again, as we slid down the back of a wave, it would explode into great walls of foam on either side of the bow.

That made me go inside and slam the door, and as I gazed out toward the north, I saw brooding black clouds on the horizon. That was not a good omen, I told myself, then dismissed the thought as stupid superstition. I found a seat and lowered myself into it, wondering absently how much the Abrahamic religions and African and native Indian tribal religions had fused and blended here—how much superstition was a part of local culture.

The trip took a little over four and a half hours, and though the threatened storm seemed to dissipate, as we approached the port of Santa Maria, there were still heavy clouds on the northern horizon, and overhead, looking oddly incongruous, a few heavy dark clouds sagged in an otherwise beautiful, clear sky.

The port was a natural cove at the end of a long spit of rock that stretched out into the sea from the main body of the island. At some point, somebody had bothered to cover the place in concrete and build two piers at right angles to each other with a narrow gap left open as an entrance to the harbor. It looked like it might have been a busy place back in the middle of last century, but right now it was all but dead. There were a couple of sailing yachts there, an old schooner, and another ferry similar to the St. Homer. Aside from that, there was little going on.

The port itself was made up of an office that had a sign over the door reading *Port Authority*. The doors and windows were closed and looked like they hadn't been open for a while. There were also a couple of bars and a scattering of houses ranging from very basic dwellings to three-story colonials that were either dilapidated but still elegant or still elegant but dilapidated, depending on whether your glass was half full or half empty.

I grabbed my bags and made my way to the ramp, where I asked one of the sailors where the car rental was. He chewed gum—or something—at me a moment like I must be stupid, then pointed ashore.

"In dah bah," he said. "*Maison La Virgen*."

I didn't bother to thank him. I carried my two Gladstone bags along the quay to the decked terrace of a large, rambling structure. It was set between an empty lot that housed a Mexican palm tree, a Brazilian flame tree, six tires, the remains of a diesel engine and an old brass bed, and a tall, severe, double-fronted colonial building in faded yellow with sage green shutters.

I stepped inside La Virgen. It was dark and empty, but there was a guy with dreadlocks behind the bar polishing glasses. He showed me some very white teeth and asked, "How you doin'?"

"Good. The guy on the boat told me you take care of car rentals."

"He ain't wrong. You want a beer after that crossing?"

"I could use one. Maybe you could tell me how to get to Es Arenal, too. I'm booked in at the I-Takka Hotel."

He wheezed a slow laugh and kept it going till he had a glass full of beer.

"Man," he said as he set it in front of me, "you ain't never gonna get lost on this island. We got just two roads. One goes east-west from here all the way along the island, seven long miles through the Downs to the Pine Valley and up to Le Mole. That's what we call the Main Road. An' then you got a road that that goes south-north from South Faro, the Temple and the lighthouse on the cliff, past Es Arenal, all the way across the Downs to North Faro, which is another lighthouse, an' that is also on a cliff. So man, you follow a road, you come to the crossroads, an' you ain't never gonna be lost."

His laugh was infectious, and I smiled as I took a long pull on the beer. Then he wagged a big finger at me as the laugh faded. "Some people might tell you, dude, just bein' on this island, you already lost!"

As he spoke the words, the tall guy who'd been sleeping on the boat came in. Behind him I could see that a light, warm rain had started to fall. Dreadlocks was saying, "Hey! Klaus, my man! What's it gonna be? You still on beer or you moving up to vodka already?"

Klaus nodded absently at me, leaned on the bar, and reached out a hand.

"Giff me a beer, Dred." Dred was already pouring it. When he handed it over, Klaus took it with a shaking hand and drained the glass. He set it down and sighed. "Make me another," he said and smiled at me. "I am drinking myself to a better world."

"Enjoy the journey," I told him.

Outside, it had grown dark in the time it took me to answer Klaus and turn to Dred. A second after that, the heavens opened, and the pregnant clouds gave birth to a deluge. Dred was wheezing again.

"I can make you a nice grass-fed burger if you ain't in a hurry."

I drained my glass and shook my head. "I'd better make a move or I'll end up headed for a better world with Klaus here. You got the vehicles under cover?"

"Yeah, man. This gonna blow over in ten minutes."

He took me out back where he had half a dozen trucks lined up under a tin roof. The rain made a loud hiss and drummed hard on the corrugated metal. Among the vehicles was a nice black Wrangler, and I pointed to it. "Is it as good as it looks?"

He raised both hands and took a step back. "All my cars, man. All my cars I look after them like they was my babies. There ain't nothin' wrong with any of my cars. You got a problem, you come to Uncle Dred. He gonna fix it for you an' make you a happy man. You wan' a babe, you wan' a joint. All good stuff, dude, happy weed, happy babes. I don't want no problems."

"A happy car will do me for now."

"You got it, dude. That Wrangler's as happy as a truck can get. Beer's on the house. Hope to see you back again."

I paid him, slung my bags in the back, and headed off west along the Main Road: the only road. The rain was heavy, and visibility was low. The car was right-hand drive, and people on the island tended to drive on the left. I say tended because half the time they seemed to drive wherever they hell they wanted to. So I took it slow, remembering what Dred had said, that the rain would blow over in ten minutes or so. Going at twenty miles an hour and sometimes less, it took me almost fifteen minutes to reach the crossroads.

I saw practically nothing of the countryside except for the green and occasionally wooded edges of the road and the deep ditches that were draining away the sudden deluge. I didn't encounter another vehicle, either, going my way or coming head on. The road seemed to be as empty as the island.

Then, suddenly, the crossroads emerged out of the rain. I braked, hydroplaned for twelve feet, and came to a stop with my hood halfway into the intersection. I backed up and saw that Dred had not lied. There was a sign, barely visible, at the side of the road, and it said left was Es Arenal. I indicated out of habit—nobody was going to see it—and turned left.

The rain didn't stop, but it began to ease as a strong wind picked up out of the south. On my right I began to see a rocky landscape that ascended toward what looked like a dense pine forest in the distance. On my left there was a deep ditch which I could now see fed canals that intersected the waterlogged fields of corn, watermelons, and fruit trees.

And then I saw something that should not have been there. At first it looked like a bundle of sodden rags being flapped around by the wind. But as I slowed and looked harder, I saw that the bundle of rags had hair, and that too was being blown this way and that by the wind. I stopped and put my hazard lights on.

I swung down from the cab and was instantly drenched by the downpour. I grabbed a luminous triangle from the trunk and, wiping the rain from my eyes, stuck it in the road twenty feet behind the Jeep. Then I ran and scrambled down into the ditch, knee deep in sludge and water. I waded across and had real trouble getting out the other side, slipping and scrambling in the loose mud. I had to crawl out and struggle to my feet, covered in sludge. From there I ran, ankle deep in the waterlogged field, to where the large bundle lay motionless, but for the cloth and hair, whipped this way and that.

I got down on my knees beside it and started to remove the rags, wiping the water from my face as it fell. But I already knew what I was going to find. She must have been fourteen or fifteen when she was alive. She'd been pretty. She would probably have grown into a beautiful woman. She was blond and very pale of skin. Her eyes, which now stared unblinking into a gray, bellying sky, were blue.

She had contusions to her neck and face. She had been gripped hard, but she had not been strangled. There was no swelling, her tongue was not protruding, nor were her eyes bulging.

I trudged back to the ditch, brushing the rain from my eyes with my fingers. I struggled across and back up to the road and collected the luminous reflective triangle I'd placed behind the Jeep. With it in my hand, I made my way back to the body and placed it by her head so I'd be able to tell the sheriff exactly where I found her. Then, with extreme difficulty, I picked her up and slung her over my shoulder. Rigor had not set in, and she was small, but even so, a dead body is difficult to move, and the extra ninety to a hundred pounds made me sink deeper into the sodden mire and made walking a real struggle. Getting her into the ditch was difficult, getting her out of it was impossible, and in the end, I had to use the winch on the front of the truck to drag her up.

Dignity belongs to the living. There is no dignity in death, whoever you are.

By the time I'd laid her on the back seat, I was a mess, saturated and covered from head to toe in mud, and I was exhausted. I stood for a moment letting the rain rinse me off. Then I got behind the wheel and set off again for Es Arenal, the capital of the island. I had a bad feeling. I was going to have to deliver this child to the sheriff. And any sheriff worth his salt was going to put me right at the top of his list of suspects. I could not afford to get arrested, much less be investigated or go on trial. But then, as the brigadier had asked, where do you draw that pragmatic line? Neither could I let this child lie dead, neglected in a field, and drive on by, not if I was going to remain human.

The gods would have to decide. The brigadier would have said that was irony.

THREE

IT WAS ABOUT A MILE AND A HALF, AND AS THE RAIN began to ease, lights began to flicker in the distance, ahead and to my right. Then I began to see, through the misty haze of the rain, a small town maybe half a mile up ahead. The road fed straight into a central plaza that was paved in red and white. At the center there was a garden with jacaranda trees, rose bushes, and benches set around a fountain. Beside it was a statue of a guy in a tricorn hat.

The rain now stopped as suddenly as it had started. Overhead, the clouds were breaking up, and the blacktop had become steel blue with reflected light. I slowed and counted six cars around the square. The newest one was a thirty-year-old convertible Rover 216 Cabrio. The oldest was a red 1960s Buick, complete with wings. Straight ahead of me was a large, three-story colonial building with a Georgian portico over an expanding flight of seven shallow steps. The windows had green, wooden shutters, all of which were closed. It had the air of a city hall. To the left of that was a terrace of houses in varying states of disrepair.

To the right there was a butchers, and next to him was a baker. Maybe the next was a candlestick maker, but I couldn't see because at a right angle to it, obscuring the road, was another building. This building was illuminated, and light flooded out onto the sidewalk and the blacktop. It was a bar. It had a blue neon sign outside that said *The Sea Breeze* in flowing letters and a picture of a fish under the word breeze, swimming in the opposite direction. Water had obviously gotten into the wiring somewhere because the sign was flickering on and off.

There were no cars moving, so I turned the wrong way into the square and came to a stop outside the bar. I pulled the dead girl from the back seat, cradled her in my arms, and carried her to the entrance. I worked the handle with my foot, pushed the door open, and stepped inside.

It wasn't even half full, but there were more people there than I'd seen so far on the whole island. There was a guy behind the bar. He was white and blond, but he had dreadlocks to his waist that looked like they might have colonies of rodents and insects living in them. The reggaeton was throbbing in the background. The guy behind the bar stopped what he was doing because apparently he couldn't put a glass on the bar and gape at the same time.

The glass of beer was intended for one of four guys standing opposite him on this side of the bar. They were all dressed in jeans and had identical khaki shirts with epaulettes. There were three cream cowboy hats on the counter. The fourth was on its owner's head. Those four guys were staring but not gaping. Around the room there were four tables. Two were occupied by families, the other two by couples.

The guys at the bar watched me, but nobody moved or said anything. I ignored them and made my way to one of the unoccupied tables. I hooked my foot around the leg and dragged it over to the next table, kicked the chairs out of the way, and laid the limp body down. Her cold, bare feet stuck out at the end. Her jeans were caked with mud, like her blouse and her hair.

I turned and studied at the four guys at the bar. I saw that the one with the hat had a star pinned to his shirt.

"Are you gentlemen deputies? Is one of you the sheriff?" I pointed at the body. "She's not sleeping. She's dead."

The guy with the star answered. "I am the sheriff on this island. Sheriff Jeremiah Scott. These are my deputies. Who are you, and what in the name of hell have you got there?"

"I'm Harry Bauer, and this is a dead girl. I spotted her body in a field, a mile and a half up the road. She was lying face down in the mud. I have left a reflective triangle to mark the spot."

They just stared at me. I'd never seen anything like it. Outside I heard distant thunder. The barman, still holding the glass of beer, the three deputies and the sheriff, and the families and couples sitting at their tables. They all just stared.

I shifted my gaze to the gaping barman. I spoke quietly. "Can we have that fucking music off out of respect for this dead child?"

He put down the glass, closed his mouth, and hurried to turn off the reggaeton. Silence settled on the room.

"You want to take it easy there, son." It was the sheriff. "There's no call to be cursing."

"There isn't? Does anybody know who this girl is?" Nobody said anything. I said to the sheriff, "Does anybody give a damn? Are you going to look at the body? Are you going to call a doctor to certify her death, and cause of death?"

He raised an eyebrow at me. "Yeah, I'm gonna look at the body, Mr. Bauer, but I reckon you need to cool down a few degrees." He turned to one of his deputies, who was clean shaven and looking very alarmed. "Rishi, go get Doctor Brown.

Tell her…" His eyes shifted to me. "Tell her the Middleton girl has been found by a stranger. She's dead."

Rishi made for the door but stopped dead and looked back at the sheriff when I said, "Are you just going to take my word for that, or are you going to check for yourself?"

He blinked slowly. "I can see from here she's dead, Mr. Bauer. And before you start making crazy insinuations, I should remind you that right now it seems you was the last person to see her alive."

I shook my head. I reached in my jacket pocket, pulled out my ferry ticket, and stepped over to him. I held out the ticket. "I was the first person to see her dead, Sheriff. Somebody else was the last to see her alive. That ticket, and the testimony of Dred at the *Maison La Virgen,* where I rented my Jeep, should make it clear I was either at sea or at the port when this girl was murdered."

I pushed past him and between the two deputies to lean on the bar and tell the bartender, who was gaping again, "Get me a beer and a hamburger."

I heard the door slam and figured Deputy Rishi had gone to get the doctor.

"It's on me." I turned and looked. The sheriff handed me back the ticket and gave the barman the nod. He said again, "It's on me, Ned." To me he said, "Gratitude for what you done, Mr. Bauer. Most people would have driven right on by. We don't mean to be discourteous, but we don't see many outsiders on I-Takka." I noticed he pronounced it as though the T was a Th. "So we tend to be a bit suspicious. No harm done."

I raised the glass Ned had brought me. "No harm, no foul. Cheers."

"Cheers." We both drank, and as he set down his glass, he

said, "So what brings you to this remote corner of the globe, Mr. Bauer?"

I set down my own glass and arched an eyebrow at him. "That accent's not from I-Takka, Sheriff. It's not Caribbean or South American. I'd place it somewhere in the southwest of the United States. Arizona?"

He smiled and came to lean on the bar beside me. "Winslow. You can believe it or not, but I was born on the corner of Kinsley Avenue and Route 66. And you're asking me what brings an Arizona cowboy to St. Homer to become sheriff in a place that would normally have a constable."

I gave my head a little twitch that said he wasn't wrong.

"Well, it's a long story, Mr. Bauer, and maybe one day I'll tell it to you over a couple of beers, but right now it looks as though I might be investigating Maisy Middleton's homicide, so I am going to ask you again real polite, what brings you to our island?"

Thunder rolled again in the distance. At the same time, bright sunshine leaned through the window and framed black shadows across the floor.

"Curiosity," I said. "I like traveling in places off the beaten track. I was reading about Surinam and Guyana, and I-Takka came up. I thought I'd come and have a look."

"Ever been to Alaska? That's pretty remote and off the beaten track."

I sighed. "Subtlety ain't the big thing here, huh, Sheriff? Alaska is also a preferred destination for serial killers. I know that, Sheriff. I am not a serial killer, and if I were, you have two or three difficult questions to answer."

"Yeah? To me it looks like it would answer all of 'em."

"First, why the hell would I bring her here instead of leaving her where I killed her? Second, have you ever come across a serial killer whose MO included taking the body of his victim to her home or her village? Third, why the hell would I kill her in the middle of a field during a rainstorm instead of doing the job in my truck and dropping her in the sea at one of the Faros? Fourth, and maybe most important, what the hell was she doing out there, alone, in the middle of that storm? What are you suggesting, Sheriff? That I arrived on the ferry, collected my car at *Maison La Virgen,* drove here through the storm and, along the way, with visibility down to twenty or thirty yards, found this girl walking alone, in the downpour, in a light dress, picked her up, and killed her? Then what did I do, dump her in a muddy field before collecting her again and bringing her here? Then I refer you to my first three questions. And the fourth, come to that."

He grunted. "You a cop? You talk like a cop."

"No. I was a soldier. I've seen a lot of death in places off the beaten track."

"Special ops?"

I nodded once. "Where do the Middletons live?"

He jerked his head to his right, the opposite direction from the field where I had found Maisy. "Down along Beachfront Road a ways."

"How far a ways?"

"Half a mile maybe. Don't go thinking about taking them the news, Mr. Bauer. I have a job to do here, and I don't want you interfering, y'hear? You booked into a hotel?"

"The I-Takka."

"That's opposite here, on the other side of the square. I suggest you check in, get yourself a shower and some rest, and let me and the doc do our jobs."

"Do I get to eat the burger you so generously invited me to?"

He didn't get to answer that because the door opened and Rishi came in with the doc, followed by a gust of cool, rain-washed breeze.

The doc was wearing dirty jeans, a stained military shirt, and muddy walking boots. Her afro hair was tied back with a thick, black elastic band. Her skin was dark, but her features were more native Caribbean than African. She had a big, brown leather satchel in her hand which for some reason looked oddly incongruous with the jeans, the military shirt, and the afro hair.

She approached the table and stood motionless, looking down at the dead girl for a long moment. Then she stroked her cheek with the back of her fingers. She felt for a pulse in her wrist and her neck and after a moment pulled her cell from her pocket and held it to her own mouth.

"Maisy Middleton, pronounced dead at the Sea Breeze at fifteen minutes after five p.m." And she gave the date. She put her cell away and bent to examine the girl's face and throat, then her hands and fingers. "Who found her?"

"I did. She was about a mile and a half up the road, face down in the field, on the right as you're leaving the village."

She glanced at me, then down at my hands.

"May I see...?"

She trailed off because I had stepped forward, unbuttoning my sleeves and rolling them up. I held out both hands, palms down. She studied them, then my forearms, and looked over at the sheriff. He approached, frowning. She told him, "I need to do a proper examination, but you can see here, her jaw? There is a very clear imprint of what appears to be a very large right-hand fist. However strong the man is, his fist will be bruised by the bone. Also, you see the bruising to her throat? Look at her fingernails." She lifted the hand and indicated the fingertips and the nails. There was skin, flesh, and blood under them. "Whoever did this has a bruised fist and badly scratched hands and/or forearms."

The sheriff nodded a few times. "Seems to put you in the clear, Mr. Bauer."

"I told you, Sheriff. I found her. Your time of death is going to be almost impossible. It'll be some time between when I found her and when she was last seen, which will probably put me on the ferry from Georgetown." I glanced at him. "But it might also tell you what the hell a girl of her age was doing out alone, more than a mile from home, in the middle of a field in a rain storm."

"You leave that to me, Mr. Bauer. You've been more than helpful enough already."

I turned to the doctor. "Doctor Brown, if you need me, I'll be at the I-Takka Hotel, across the square."

She nodded once, examining my face with eyes that were not hostile but were definitely not friendly either. She said, "Thank you," then turned to the sheriff. "Can you have your boys load her in the back of my truck and bring her into the mortuary?" She handed over the keys and added, "I'll see you there."

She stepped outside with me. Overhead, the sky was turning to evening. I pulled open the driver's door of the Wrangler. She paused on the sidewalk and pointed to the big building I had seen on my arrival that looked to me like a city hall.

"Drive me to the town hall? It's on your way."

"Sure, get in."

She climbed in, and we slammed the doors. As I pulled away, she said, "Are you some kind of cop?"

"Straight to the point, huh? What would some kind of cop

be?" I turned to look at her. "And more to the point, whose jurisdiction would he have?"

"Are you dodging the question to avoid answering it? If so, you just answered it."

"No, I am not a cop. Why do you ask?"

She smiled. "Twice. You dodged the question twice. You're not a cop, but I asked you if you were some kind of cop."

I had pulled up outside City Hall—their town hall. It was all closed up and dark, but there was a side alley, and down there I could see the rear lights of her truck, where Maisy's body was being delivered. She opened the door and swung down. Before slamming the door, she said, "I might need you to come round tomorrow when I do the autopsy. I want you to explain some things to me."

"You want me to come in now?"

She shook her head. "Not now, tomorrow."

I nodded. "Sure."

She slammed the door, and I covered the short distance to the hotel.

FOUR

It was a slightly smaller version of what I thought of as City Hall. It had a gable roof and yellow walls with green, slatted wooden shutters. Two granite steps led up to double dark wood doors with glass panels that bore the words in gold leaf lettering *Hotel St Homer*.

I pushed through and found myself in an old world lobby with a checkerboard floor and a mahogany desk on the right with a brass bell. Ahead, two doors with what looked like genuine art deco glass panels stood open in an arched doorway. Beyond them I could see a dining room which had probably been elegant a hundred years earlier. There were a couple of potted palms by the arch and then on my left an elegant mahogany staircase spiraled to the upper floors. I dropped my bags on the floor and rang the bell.

She emerged after a moment from an office behind the desk. She had dark hair and dark eyes and a body that was slim but generous. She came forward frowning, like somehow I didn't make sense. I smiled and arched an eyebrow.

"It said hotel on the door..."

She gave a little start and clenched her hands in front of her womb. "Oh, you're..." She didn't finish, like the words had gotten stuck crosswise in her throat.

"Not yet," I said, "but I hope to be. This *is* the I-Takka hotel, though on the door it says St. Homer?"

"Yes," she said and then nodded a couple of times, like she was confirming it to herself. "We changed the name when we bought the hotel, but getting the glass changed was not as easy as we... Did you have an accident? Do you need a doctor or a mechanic?"

I looked down at myself. "Yeah, I see what you mean. No. I just need a shower and a change of clothes. There was a—" I gestured at the door.

She said, "You didn't book, I imagine?"

"I was told it wouldn't be necessary at this time of year. But I'll take the biggest, most comfortable room you've got."

"Oh," she said, opening a large, red book of the sort you see in old movies. "That would be the Sugar Cane Suite. Perhaps you'd like some..." She trailed off, looking at my clothes. "Perhaps you'd like a drink and some lunch while Camilla prepares your room?"

We arranged in the end that I would shower and change, and Camilla would fix up the room when I was done, and I would have a martini and a steak to make up for the burger I didn't get to eat at the Sea Breeze.

She had the table ready for me when I came down. It was set with white linen and a linen napkin. Both were a little frayed, but they had been bleached and pressed, and the glasses and the cutlery were glistening in the slightly subdued light. I even had a candle on the table. I was also alone in the dining room.

As I sat, she came in through an arch that I figured led to

the kitchen and possibly a bar. She seemed nervous, like she wasn't accustomed to having guests. "What can I get you? Will you have a drink while you wait?"

"I'll have a martini, dry, gin with an olive."

"Of course." Again the nervous smile, and she handed me the menu. "I'm afraid there are no specials today."

She left, probably in the direction of the bar, with the air of a woman who's managed a difficult task. I opened the menu. I was taking a second look at the starters when I sensed a presence at the door. The girl there was too attractive to be almost half my age, but she wasn't a day over nineteen and definitely way too attractive. Leaning on the doorjamb, she smiled with all the ease the manageress lacked.

"Hi," she said and paused.

"Hi..."

"I'm Camilla, Marguerite's daughter."

"Marguerite...?"

"The lady who's fixing your martini in the bar and cooking your dinner in the kitchen. She's an all-rounder, like me. She's my mom." She laughed, and it was almost infectious. It made me smile. "I just wanted to say hi, and if there's anything you need, you only have to ask. I'm just going up to do your suite." She pointed at the menu. "Shoulder of suckling lamb. It is like totally fresh, slaughtered this morning. The starters, I'd recommend the smoked salmon with avocado?" She said it like it was a question, but somehow it wasn't annoying. "The prawns, oysters, all that stuff is frozen. We don't get it fresh this time of year."

"Thanks for the heads up."

She hesitated a moment, like she was going to add something, then smiled, said, "Yeah," and went upstairs.

Marguerite brought my drink, I gave her my order, and

fifteen minutes later, she brought me the smoked salmon and avocado and a glass of very cold white wine. She set them down and hesitated. I smiled up at her as I shook open the napkin.

"Marguerite," I said. "Something is on your mind."

"Well..."

"Why don't you sit down and tell me?"

"I don't want to intrude on your meal..."

"You're not. Sit down. Is it about the girl I found by the road?"

She sat very slowly, with her hands clenched in front of her. When she spoke, it was almost a whisper.

"Yes..."

"She was murdered." It was brutal, but something inside told me we could get stuck for eternity in her oversensitive dithering. "The sheriff didn't seem awful surprised."

"Murdered? How...?" She trailed off.

"We'll have a better idea once the doc has done an autopsy, but it was clear she'd been beaten. She had pretty bad bruising."

She didn't say anything. I continued eating, then asked, "Has this happened before?"

She still didn't answer. I looked up from my food. She was staring at me.

"No." She drew breath, hesitated, and shook her head. "No."

I smiled, wiped my mouth, and dropped my napkin beside my plate.

"That's a no that says 'Yes, but it's too complicated to explain.' Am I wrong?"

She closed her eyes and took a deep breath. It wasn't exactly a sigh. It was more like an expression of weariness.

"No," she said at last. "You're not wrong, but you are also

right in that it is too complicated to explain. And..." She gestured at me with both hands and forced a smile. "You are on holiday. I am sorry you had such a distressing experience on arriving."

She went to reach for my plate. I spoke quietly as I picked up my glass of wine.

"I was eight years with the British Special Air Service. I've served in Iraq, Afghanistan, Colombia, Mexico, and other places I can't mention. In eight years of active service, you see a lot of things. You see a lot of human suffering. You see a lot of fear and a lot of courage." I paused, watching her, before going on. "Courage—extreme courage—can express itself in different ways in men and women. Sometimes, especially among women, it can be real quiet. Sometimes it can even look like fear. There comes a point when you start to recognize it. You walk into a room, a house, a village, anywhere where there's a group of people, and you can smell it."

She was staring at the tablecloth. When I finished, she reached across the table for my plate. As she took hold of it, I said, "I can smell it here. It stinks. Tell me what's so complicated about what happened before."

She froze. I waited. After a couple of seconds, she picked up my plate and said, "I'll go and get your lamb."

She was gone a good five minutes while I finished my wine. In my mind, I could see the child lying face down in the mud, her sodden hair flapping this way and that. I could see the doc talking to the sheriff, pointing to the child's jaw: "...you can see here, her jaw? There is a very clear imprint of what appears to be a medium-sized right hand fist..."

One part of my mind questioned if her murder had anything to do with the reason I was there or whether it was just a bizarre coincidence. Another kept telling me she shouldn't have been lying face down in the mud.

She should not have been face down in the mud.

Marguerite came out of the kitchen with a sizzling shoulder of lamb and placed it in front of me. The smell was intense. Rosemary, honey, garlic.

"Will you have a glass of house red with that? The house red is actually quite good."

I smiled on the right side of my face. The brigadier would approve. Not only did she suggest a red wine with lamb, she could do it following a discussion about a recent murder. This woman had hidden depths.

"Yes, I would," I said. "I'll tell you what, Marguerite, why don't you bring a bottle and two glasses, take a seat, and call me Harry?"

She stood frozen, staring at me. I waited, watching her, until the situation and the silence became too embarrassing and she nodded and hurried away. She came back a while later with a newly opened bottle of *Casillero del Diablo* and poured me a glass, muttering something about its not having breathed. I watched her face while she did it. When she stopped pouring, I gestured at the seat opposite me, where she'd been sitting before.

"I hope you don't mind if I eat while we talk. This smells delicious."

I picked up my knife and fork, and somehow that made it a *fait accompli*. She sighed, poured herself a glass of wine, and sat.

"I really should be cleaning the kitchen, Mr. Bauer."

"Harry." I tasted the lamb. It really was very good, and I told her so. Then I leaned back in my chair and sipped the wine. That was good too.

"So what happened before, and why is it so hard to explain?"

She studied me a moment. "Are you a policeman?"

"People keep asking me that. It's my understanding both Surinam and Guyana have unofficially abdicated from running this island. As far as I can see, the only authority here is Sheriff Scott, and he's not even an islander." She waited. I said, "No, I am not a cop. Who would send a cop here? Not Surinam, not Guyana. So who? I'm just a guy who has seen too many children and vulnerable people get killed by bullies. Maisy Middleton was a fourteen- or fifteen-year-old child. Now she no longer exists, and her parents have been destroyed. Do you know who did this?"

"No, of course not."

"This has a precedent. It's happened before, or something very like it. It reeks off everyone I speak to, from the barman at the Sea Breeze, to the sheriff, to the doc, and to you. I can see it on your faces and hear it in your voices. You have seen this before, and you are scared."

She closed her eyes again. "*All right*, Mr. Bauer!"

"Harry."

She sighed. "Harry... Yes, something similar happened before. A young girl was murdered. Sally. Sally Haight. She was beaten, then stabbed. Her body was found in the woods in Pine Valley, near the Cala."

"Stabbed?"

"Yes, in the lower belly. Caroline—that's the doctor—she said she had been stabbed many times with a long, thin blade."

I spoke half to myself, staring at the lamb without seeing it. "But there was no blood at the scene, where they found her."

I shifted my eyes from the lamb to her face and saw that she had gone pale. Her voice was very quiet when she asked, "How would you know that?"

I frowned, running it through my mind. "Because Maisy was lying face down. What caught my eye was her hair being whipped up by the wind. But she had been punched hard in the jaw. That would knock a small girl like Maisy on her back. But then, when the doc was examining the body, there was skin under her nails where she'd scratched her assailant, skin and blood, but no mud. And when I picked her up, there was no blood. Not on her blouse, not on the ground."

She had her brows contracted. "I don't understand what you're getting at. What are you trying to say?"

"She wasn't killed in that field, just like Sally wasn't killed at the beach. They were both killed somewhere else, then dumped."

"How can you be so sure of that?"

"I'm not, but my gut is. And my gut is never wrong. Have you got Doctor Scott's number?"

"Yes..."

"You mind giving it to me?" I saw her do her hesitating again, so I cut her short and said, "OK, just call her. Ask her if she's still at the morgue. Tell her I want to see her now. While you do that, I'm going to finish this lamb. It's good."

She narrowed her eyes, and after a moment, while I sat and chewed, she made the call on her cell.

"Caroline, it's Marguerite. I have Mr. Bauer staying with me. He is dining, and he asked me to call you..." She listened for a moment, then went on. "The lamb, yes it's very fresh. He is very kind about it. No...not this time of year. The smoked salmon..."

I cleared my throat. She glanced at me.

"Listen, Caroline, Mr. Bauer wondered if you were still at

the morgue. He would like to see you as soon as possible." She looked across the table at me and nodded. "You'll wait for him? Super. He'll be very pleased. Bye, Caroline. Take care."

She hung up.

"She was finishing up for the evening, but she'll wait for you. The entrance is down the side ally on the right as you face the door."

I had cleaned the bone and now I drained my glass. "That's great. What did she have for dinner?"

Her eyes widened. "I didn't ask."

I stood and smiled. And they say it's us Yanks who don't understand irony. "I won't be long. Don't lock me out."

I stepped out onto that damp sidewalk. Slick puddles of streetlight lay across the black, and a low moon was touching broken clouds with turquoise light. My footsteps echoed loudly as I crossed the square to City Hall and became oddly muffled as I slipped into the alley and made for the door that stood ajar in the walling, spilling amber light.

I slipped through and closed the door behind me. Something told me it was as well nobody found me here talking to the doc.

I found myself in a small anteroom with corridors branching right and left into darkness. Ahead, three bare concrete steps led down to a short passage where light was glowing through a set of double fire doors. I went down and pushed through into a large room with a couple of steel autopsy tables. One of them held Maisy's pallid body, covered in a sheet. There were half a dozen refrigerator drawers in the left-hand wall. Not many people died here, I guessed, because not many lived here.

Doctor Caroline Brown was leaning against a bench on my right beside a sink, a kettle, and a mug. She'd covered her military shirt with a lab coat and looked almost like a medical examiner. She was watching me.

“How much did you get out of her?” she said. “Not much, I’m willing to bet.”

I gave my head a small shake, then pointed at Maisy’s body. “She was stabbed in the lower belly?” She nodded. I said, “There was no blood on her blouse or on the ground. She wasn’t killed in the field. She was dumped there.” She nodded again, slowly and ponderously. I said, “Like Sally Haight.”

“Yes,” she said. “Like Sally.”

FIVE

"How many have there been?"

She reached in the pocket of her lab coat and pulled out a pack of Camels. She lit up with a match and took a long draw, then inhaled deeply through her mouth, squinting at me as she did so.

"Not a cop, huh?"

I frowned. "I'm not a cop, Doc. But I'm going to ask you the same question I asked you before. If I were, who would I be working for?"

She shrugged and flicked ash on the floor. "I don't know. We get a lot of weird people here. Mostly Americans. They all behave as though they own the island."

"Weird how?"

She smiled, like a touch of humor would make what she was going to say a little less offensive. "Weird like you. I don't mean to be offensive."

I dismissed her apology with a shake of my head. What she'd said made sense if the brigadier's intelligence was right. I walked over to Maisy's body and pulled back the sheet. The stab wounds were there, in the lower belly. It was hard to make out how many without a close inspection, as they crossed and overlapped each other.

"A frenzy," I said.

"Twelve," she said. "With a long, slim blade. The same as Sally."

"And there was no earth or mud in her mouth or in her nose."

"No."

"So she wasn't breathing when she went face down."

"She was already dead. But you already knew that because there was no blood where you found her or on her blouse."

I stared down at her childlike face, trying not to think about what she had felt or thought in her last minutes of life. "He punched her, removed her blouse, went into his frenzy, and when she had bled out, he put her blouse back on, took her to that field, and dumped her."

"I can't see another explanation."

"How long ago was Sally?" I turned to face her. She was flicking ash with her right ring finger, though there was none accumulated on the coal. "Two months." She said it to her cigarette.

"And before that?"

Now she looked up, curious. "How do you know there was one before that?"

"Because this is a serial killer, and he already had his method established when he killed Sally. So it's a better than average chance that he had done it before."

She shrugged. "Yeah. Six months earlier. Madeleine Vasco. The beating was more extensive, and the stabbing was more random. There were overhand stabs to the chest, her arms were cut, and the stab wounds to the belly were more widely spaced."

She took a pull on her cigarette and blew out a long stream while she stubbed it out.

"You know a lot about bodies for a guy who's not a homicide cop. What do you do, watch a lot of CSI?"

"All the reruns."

"You're not telling, huh?"

"There's nothing to tell. I was in special ops. You get to see a lot of bodies, and you learn to read them."

She nodded like it made sense to her, then asked, "What are you dong here, Harry?"

I studied her a moment, her smart, knowing eyes, her slippers and lab coat, her big hair tied behind her head. I wondered how much she knew, how useful it would be to confide in her, and how risky it would be.

"I came to the remotest place on the planet, trying to get away from it all."

"Well, that's one hell of a coincidence, huh?"

She turned, opened a cabinet, and pulled out a bottle of Bells and two shot glasses.

"What is?"

"You, a retired American special ops soldier who talks like a homicide detective, showing up here just when our mystery serial killer starts taking out girls, and just six months after the Company arrives."

I watched her pour two measures, and as she handed me one, I asked, "The Company?"

She arched an eyebrow. "Oh, you didn't know about the Company? You know about everything else, I thought you'd know about that, too." She knocked back the shot and refilled her glass.

"I assume you're not talking about the CIA. So who is the Company?"

"I have no idea. Maybe it is the CIA. Maybe it's a branch of Area 51. We just call them the Company. They keep to themselves. They built a..."—she shrugged and spread her hands—"base? Facility? Factory? Whatever it is, it's big, and it's surrounded by barbed wire and fifteen-foot walls, and it's guarded by men with uniforms and machine guns. At first people were happy. They thought it would bring jobs to the island."

"And did it?" I knocked back the shot, and she handed me the bottle.

"Oh, sure. When they opened up, they recruited three hundred people. That's a lot of people on this island. They took all sorts, but mainly families."

"*Families?*"

She nodded slowly, using her whole body in each nod. "Uh-huh. They said the work they were doing was classified. And they paid exceptional wages and provided food and accommodation, but the condition was, you signed up for at least a year, and you never left the site. Why would you want to? That's what they asked. You have restaurants, pools, cinema, doctors, even a small hospital—everything you might need. Sign up for a year or two, and bring your whole family! Three hundred people signed up, and we haven't seen them since." She laughed suddenly. "And like you keep pointing out, who are we going to tell? If we report it to Surinam, they say it's Guyana's problem. We report it to Guyana, it's Surinam's problem. But in any case, how are we going to report it? Through the sheriff? Through the mayor? They're the guys who brought them here in the first place."

"Wait, what do you mean?"

"Sheriff Scott introduced the directors of the Company to Eric Olafsen, the mayor. He just showed up one day, had some meeting with the mayor, brought over a bunch of guys in suits in a helicopter, and next thing they started building that thing, whatever it is. Next thing after that, the mayor announces we are doing away with the old constable system we'd had since the British Empire and instituting a new sheriff system because it was more democratic. And he went and 'democratically'"—she made inverted comma signs with her fingers—"appointed Sheriff Jeremiah Scott."

I sat on a small plastic chair and was quiet for a while, running over everything in my mind. Eventually she reached out and took the bottle and the glass from my hands and poured me another shot.

"Who else have you spoken to about this?"

"Nobody. You sometimes get some of the old guys mumbling about it when they're drunk. We ignore them, like they're talking crazy. But we all know it's there. It's the elephant in the room, only it's wearing a rifle round its neck. So you just keep right on pretending it ain't there."

"So why are you telling me?"

She put a smile on her right cheek. It looked cute. I knocked back the shot and returned the smile.

"You didn't exactly show up like one of those occasional backpacking gap year kids who land here from time to time or those sporadic adventure holiday couples who arrive every August. Here's this guy who looks like he eats concrete for breakfast and sharpens knives on his forearms, turns up talking like a homicide cop, turns out he's special forces and to cap it all, he gives a damn. I figure I might risk it." She gave a small laugh and fished her pack of Camels out of her pocket. "And I'll tell you something else, Mr. Special Ops. I ain't as stupid as

I look. Any normal man, even a good man, around about where I used the word 'Company' or 'barbed wire' would have told me he wished me well and he'd see what he could do from back home, and he would have been out of here." She lit up and pointed at me as she removed a piece of tobacco from her lower lip. "You? You just keep asking pertinent questions..."—she paused with an ironic smile on her face—"just like it all meant something to you."

I grunted and handed her my glass. She took it and said, "Right?" And putting on a generic redneck accent, she added, "It don't do t'underestimate the village doc, Mr. Special Ops."

"Clearly."

"So why are you here, Harry?"

She refilled my glass and handed it over. I took it and knocked it back. I felt the warmth go down and narrowed my eyes at her. "Eats concrete for breakfast and sharpens knives on his forearms?"

"Don't dodge the question, big guy."

"I don't aim to. I have had one whisky too many, and I am tired after a very long journey. I am going to go to my room and think and try to sleep. I will talk to you tomorrow. The next bottle of whisky is on me."

"You know it."

I stood, and as I moved for the door, she said, "How're they treating you at the St. Homer? Marguerite and Camilla being good to you?"

There was a humor in her voice and in her eyes that made me stop and look at her. "Yeah," I said. "So far so good."

"See you tomorrow, big guy. Be good, and if not, you know, be careful."

I nodded. "You too."

When I got back to the hotel, there was no one around, but

my key was lying on the counter with a note that said simply, 'Mr. Bauer.' I went up to my room, had another shower and brushed my teeth, and fell onto the bed and from there into a deep sleep.

AT BREAKFAST THE NEXT MORNING, I asked Marguerite where I could find the sheriff. She told me his office was at the back of City Hall. I took a stroll across the square and down the alley past the morgue where I had been the night before with Doc Caroline Brown. It led me to a broad street with houses that had once been elegant, set back from the road among lawns and gardens. On my left, directly behind City Hall, was a sprawling, one-story building with a large parking lot. It had a blue lamp over the entrance and a sign that said *Police Station*.

I crossed over and pushed through the doors. It was a lot more like an English police station than a sheriff's office. There was a counter, like a shop. Behind it, Deputy Rishi was sitting reading the *St. Homer Times*. The front page headline said the Georgetown ferry had been delayed two hours because of a storm. He looked up at me and smiled.

"Good morning, Mr. Bauer. How can I be of assistance?"

"I need to see the sheriff," I told him.

"Oh, he's not here. Can I help?"

"No. I need to see him. Where is he?"

"Well—" He shifted his head from side to side, like that wasn't such a simple question to answer. "He is up at South Faro, at the temple."

The word made me squint and arch an eyebrow at the same time. "*Temple?*"

He gave a laugh that would have suited a twelve year-old

with hormones. "Oh, gosh, yes, you see, foreigners get confused. But before, with the sugar plantations, there were lots of people here, and so much coming and going, and so many religions. But you know, all basically the same: Believe in God, don't kill, don't steal, and don't have sex with your neighbor's wife or husband."

"Right..."

"So the governor, who was British, but also Portuguese, he said on the island we will have one church. We call it the Temple of God, and here all people will pray together on Sunday. But too many people!" He laughed again. "So there is one on North Faro too, Sandy Cove and Santa Maria, but the big one is on South Far. The governor, Joseph Santa Maria, he said the Temple should be by the lighthouse, because the light shows the way to God."

My smile failed to convince my eyes to join in. I said, "Deep," but I didn't mean it. "So the sheriff is up at the Temple? It's not Sunday."

"They have taken poor Maisy. There will be a service for her tomorrow and then the funeral. The cemetery and the tanatorio are also by the Temple."

I nodded for a few seconds, with a hot anger building in my gut. I said, "Tanatorio?"

"Oh, yes, we call it this. The crematorium."

"Thanks. Left out of the village, right?"

"Indeed."

I stopped at the morgue on my way back to the square. It was dark and locked up. I made my way to where the Wrangler was parked outside the hotel headed out of the village under a clear blue sky. I could now see clearly what had been hidden from view by the rain the day before, and I paused at the intersection to have a look. The fields ahead and to my right were still saturated and muddy. They were flat for maybe half a mile or a little more, and after that, the ground began to rise into what they called the Downs, rolling green hills that would not have looked out of place in rural Virginia or Sussex in England.

To my left, the hills rose toward the North Faro cliffs, and beyond them, farther west the three wooded hills that just about made it to mountain status. The Mole was the largest by height and volume and was smothered in dense pine forest. Just north of the Mole was North Mole, known locally, I was told, as Tetachika, also densely forested. Between them lay Pine Valley, which as the name suggests carried the pine forest from one Mole to the next. Slightly to the north and east of those two mountains stood the smaller Monte Faro, where the island's third lighthouse stood. Between it and North Mole lay the Sandy Cove, where the Main Road ended and the beach was reputedly superb.

I spun the wheel and turned left, accelerating toward South Faro. Pretty soon, all the abundant greenery of the center and western end of the island began to fall away, and I found myself climbing steadily through red rocks and sparse vegetation toward a series of stark, weird silhouettes on the rocky, rusty horizon. As I drew closer, those silhouettes began to resolve themselves into the tall, gabled shape of a church with a tall spire with a stark cross towering above it. To the right of that was the long, low shape of the crematorium with its tall, sinister chimney, and just beyond that the startling, surreal shape of a giant satellite dish aerial.

SIX

THERE WAS A BLUSTERY WIND COMING IN OFF THE sea from the east. I was high above the ocean on the cliff, but the wind carried the sigh and crash of the waves down below, along with the smell of salt and spray.

The Temple was surprisingly massive and rose stark, sudden, and white out of the rusty, iron rocks. It could have been a church in Mexico or even Spain or Portugal. It struck me suddenly, as I swung down from the Wrangler, that that was the nature of this island. It had no identity, no soul of its own. Maybe that was what Joseph Santa Maria had understood when he had that temple built.

The sheriff's truck was parked outside. Beside it was an old Cherokee, and beside that a brand, spanking new Range Rover. I climbed the three broad, shallow steps to the porch and stepped from the bright sunshine into the shadows. The floor was painted oxblood red, and the large oak doors stood open in the stone gothic archway. For a moment, beyond the archway there was only darkness, but I could hear the soft, rolling echo of voices.

I stepped through the arch, and the voices stopped and seemed to roll away into the shadows and the corners. The nave was maybe forty or fifty yards—sixty or more to the sanctuary—with an aisle down each side, separated from the nave by nine arches supported on marble columns. The only light came from thirteen candles that were set around the altar, four on either side and five at the back. There was a massive, wooden cross, easily twelve feet high, in the apse at the back of the altar, but there was no figure of Christ on it. Behind the cross there was a strikingly beautiful stained glass window depicting what I took to be the Ascension. The glass was predominantly a deep, vibrant blue with gold and red in the robes of the eleven remaining Apostles.

The only light was that coming through the stained glass and from the candles. In that light, I could see the sheriff watching me. With him were a priest in a black robe, a lanky guy in a badly cut suit, a big man in a waistcoat and a tweed jacket, and Doctor Caroline Brown. Beyond them was what looked like an altar boy in a red robe, kneeling on the steps to the altar, chanting softly to himself.

I stood staring at them a moment, aware they could only see my silhouette against the bright daylight behind me. The priest lifted his chin, and a rich, elegant English voice echoed among the arched shadows.

"Who's there? I am Father João. Can I help you?"

I didn't answer, but I began to walk toward them, hearing my own steps bounce off the walls around me. When I was ten paces away, I spoke, and my voice sounded loud and resonated.

"Sheriff, we need to talk."

The big guy in the vest and the Harris tweed boomed, "Who are you? You have been asked. Who are you?"

I drew level with them. The doc didn't greet me. She was

too busy watching the sheriff. I held the sheriff's eye for a slow count of three. Then I turned and looked at the big guy. He was easily six three, in his fifties, with gray hair swept back in what he probably thought was a leonine mane. I asked him, "Are you the sheriff?"

He frowned like I'd spoken to him in a dead language. "Of course I'm not! I—"

He was going to carry on, but I cut him short. "Then I don't need to talk to you."

His mouth shut with a pop, and I turned back to the sheriff. "You got a moment?"

He glanced at the other four. The priest, a small man with big hands and feet, who I now noticed had no dog collar, said, "Please, we can wait." The lanky guy nodded.

The sheriff led the way back down the nave and out into the sunshine. He made for his truck, where he leaned his back against the hood and crossed his arms. His expression asked me what it was about. He didn't speak. I studied his face a moment, then asked, "You need permission to talk to me?"

There was anger in his eyes, but he spoke quietly. "Them folk in there are the mayor and Joseph Santa Maria, the governor of the island."

"And you need their permission to talk to me."

"What do you want, Mr. Bauer?"

"Where is Maisy Middleton's body?"

His frown deepened, and his voice rose. "That's none of your goddamn business."

"Did you bring her here?"

"I told you—"

"I want to pay my last respects. What's got you so hostile, Sheriff?"

He balked, hesitating. "Your attitude ain't helping."

"I didn't know I had an attitude. Is she here?"

"She's inside."

"Did the doctor tell you what she found last night?" He didn't answer. I repeated the question. "Did she tell you what she found, Sheriff?"

"Found? Where? What are you talking about?"

"The stab wounds in the lower belly, the absence of blood, the skin and blood under her nails, the fact that there was no mud or dirt in her mouth or her nose."

"That's—"

"It means Maisy was killed somewhere else, in a frenzy. Then her body was dumped in the field. Does that ring any bells for you, Sheriff?"

"Now you listen to me, Bauer!"

"How about Sally Haight and Madeleine Vasco?"

"I've just about—"

"You have a serial killer on your island, Sheriff." I pointed over at the Temple. "And you are about to incinerate the evidence. You want to explain that to me? Or have you had just about enough?"

His voice was real quiet when he answered. "You better get out of my face, Bauer."

"I'll get out of your face when you explain to me why, on an island with practically no tourism, the presence of a serial killer who preys on young girls is being suppressed. If you're not hiding it from potential tourists, who the hell are you hiding it from? Tell me this too, Sheriff. Could it have anything to do with the Company? Could it have anything to do with the three hundred people who went missing when you and your friends the defense contractors arrived?"

The anger drained from his face and was replaced with a sneer.

"Boy, you are so out of your depth you are all but drowned."

"That's all I wanted, Sheriff." His face said he didn't know what I was talking about. I leaned a little closer and whispered the word "*Confirmation.*"

Now he looked worried. A voice from the Temple door made him look. It was the big guy. The lanky one and the doc stood behind him.

"Mr. Bauer, will your business take long? We are engaged in important matters."

I studied him a moment. I didn't think the mayor of this island would wear a thousand dollar Harris tweed. So this was the governor. The lanky, Nordic looking guy behind him, that was the mayor. I turned back to Sheriff Scott.

"No," I said, looking him in the eye. "We're done." I turned and approached the small group. "But I want to pay my respects to Maisy Middleton. Where is she?"

They all looked at Father da Silva. His face was rigid, but his eyes were mad. After a couple of seconds, he placed a transparent smile where a snarl should have been and gestured toward the Temple doors.

"Of course," he said. "Follow the left aisle past the North Transept and the vestry. You'll find there is a meditation room behind the altar. There she is laid to receive the Lord's grace before her ascension."

I nodded and pushed past him, between him and the doc. At the first step, he called after me, "Mr. Bauer!" I stopped and looked back. "The akolouthos are there, in reflection and meditation, keeping her company in her last hours on Earth. Please don't disturb them."

"I won't disturb your akolouthos, Father."

I felt their eyes on me all the way up to the door. They didn't say a word.

In the dark vault of the nave, I crossed to the left aisle and followed it through quiet, shaded echoes to the North Transept. I paused to look at a stained glass window at the end, in the same intense blue as the one behind the altar, that showed St. Peter crucified upside down. I moved on through the vestry and came finally to a plain stone arch supported by a black pillar on my right and a white pillar on my left. I tried to remember what I had read once about secret cults representing the pillars of Solomon's temple as black and white, but I thought it was the other way around. Boaz, the left pillar, was represented as black.

I told myself I was overthinking it and stepped through.

What I saw made me think again. Her body was not in a casket. It lay on a table. She was dressed in a white robe, and she and the table were strewn with flowers. The brigadier would have said she looked pre-Raphaelite, only her eyes were open and staring unseeing at the ceiling, giving her an appearance of paralyzed terror.

Seated around her on hard bentwood chairs were twelve boys, three in each of the cardinal points. They were dressed in red robes with yellow sashes and blue caps. Some had their eyes closed; others were just staring at the corpse. I estimated their ages at between ten and twelve years old, and each one of them had a hideously disfigured face. One had only one eye, placed too high on his forehead. Another had the left side of his head and face caved in, and a third had a large hole where his right eye and cheekbone should have been, so you could see right through him.

They ignored me as I stood looking, first at them and then at Maisy's corpse. I told myself it was not her. It was just a suit she had left behind. I told myself a child's soul must find peace when the body dies too soon. But in my bones I knew these were anesthetic words I was feeding myself to take away the brutal pain of the truth, that some bastard had dragged this child to hell before murdering her, that if there was such a thing as a soul, this poor child was still remembering her own horrific death, and here, in this nightmare chamber, her body was now being defiled in this insane ritual.

I left the room and made my way back through the Temple. The nave was empty, but as I approached the doors, out in the sunshine, I could see their silhouetted forms gathered at the sheriff's truck, where I had left them. They were talking in hushed voices, but they fell silent as I stepped out.

I approached them on the way to my Jeep, stopped, and pointed at the tall, lanky Scandinavian-looking guy. "Eric Olafsen, the mayor of St. Homer, I-Takka." I eyed the doc. She looked worried. "Doctor Caroline Brown." I pointed at the big guy with the leonine head and said, "And the governor, Joseph Santa Maria. The cabal, right?" Santa Maria's eyes narrowed. I shook my head. "No, Olafsen, the doc and Sheriff Scott are just pawns, aren't they? Tools. They don't count. Your boys that count, they're in D.C. and Virginia, aren't they, Joe?"

"You are a very stupid man, Mr. Bauer."

"You think so? I haven't survived this long by being stupid, Joe. I want a chat with you and your cabal at the Company offices, Joe. I'll be waiting for your invitation."

His lip curled, and he spat the words, "I don't think so!"

I smiled. "You know why people keep things secret, Joe?" I leaned toward him. "Because they're scared. However powerful you think you are, pal, you are pissing in your pants. But I'm not hiding, Joe. I'm out in the open, and I'm telling you here and now, all of you, I am coming for you. And anyone—

anyone—who was involved in those girls' killings, or protecting their killer, I will kill him, and I will kill you. An eye for an eye. A life for a life."

I climbed into my truck and pulled away. They watched me drive, not back the way I had come but past the entrance to the crematorium, fronted by a broad lawn and tall palms and the word *Tanatorio* over the plate glass entrance in large black letters. A little after that, I came to a large steel gate set in a barbed wire fence. Beyond it, maybe a hundred yards away or a little more, was a huge satellite dish aimed at the sky. It was incongruous, bizarrely out of place, and I had no doubt at all it had everything to do with the Company, the Pentagon's defense contractors.

I drove on by like I wasn't interested and headed for the road that led back to town. The colonel would have said I was reckless. Maybe she'd be right. Maybe I was. But Joseph and the sheriff knew I was making a point when I told them people who keep secrets are scared; people who are out in the open are not. They knew I was making the point that I represented somebody powerful, and taking me out would be stupid because it would draw unwanted attention and retribution. So they needed to be careful: I knew it, and they knew it. I was sure they were asking themselves if I was bluffing, but as long as they weren't sure, they could not afford to take the risk.

Their next move, I told myself, would be to invite me to meet the cabal at the Company compound and try to pump me or negotiate with me. Then I would know who they were, and I would make good on my promise. I would kill them. I didn't know yet what the connection was between the girls' deaths and the lithium mine, but I meant to find out, and I knew exactly who was going to tell me.

There are all kinds of sayings that cover it, from Joseph

Heller's "Nothing ever works as planned" to the old Yiddish "We plan, God laughs." Take your pick; for me, they both nailed it.

I was approaching the fork in the road where left would take me to the crossroads and right would take me through the fields and into Es Arenal. I slowed, pulled over to the side of the road, and killed the engine. I figured I knew enough to let the brigadier know where I was at; I also had a feeling I might need him on standby. I didn't think the sheriff and Eric Olafsen were going to be representative of the people I was going up against. I had a hunch the people at the Company were going to be of a very different caliber. I didn't often call for backup, but I was beginning to think I could use a couple of Blades with me on this one.

I pulled my cell from my pocket and saw there was no signal. In my mind, I could see the big antenna on the cliff, looking up at the satellites beyond the clear blue sky.

"Son of a bitch," I said quietly to myself.

Either they were already hunting me, or hunting and killing me was plan B, and they were preparing the ground.

I fired up the truck and drove sedately back to the hotel. Cobra had an emergency landline number for situations like this, where you couldn't use the secure Cobra cells. I parked out front and pushed into the lobby. Marguerite was behind the counter writing in a ledger. She looked up but didn't look happy when she saw me, even though I gave her my best 'I'm about to kill everyone on your island' smile.

"Mr. Bauer, good morning."

"Do you often lose signal on the island?"

She looked vaguely surprised. "No, never that I can recall."

"Do you have a landline I can use? I need to check in at the office. If they don't hear from me, they start to worry."

"Of course. Down the passage here on the right." She pointed with her pen. "It's an antique, but it works."

It was an old, mahogany, soundproofed cubicle complete with a red leather seat. The telephone itself had been updated around about the end of the Second World War, but when I lifted the receiver, I got a dial tone.

I put in the number as fast as I could with the rotating dial, and after a moment, I heard it ring at the other end. It rang once, and a girl's sing-song voice said, "Universal Solutions, how may I direct your call?"

"Hi, this is Harry Bauer. I need to talk to the manager."

There was a pause while she checked voice recognition. Then she said, "Putting you through."

Two beats and the brigadier said, "Harry."

"Hey, Pete, cells are down here, so I'm calling from a landline at my hotel." I laughed, "The I-Takka or St. Homer, take your pick. Listen, I was thinking about your offer. It's been good to just have a couple of days to think it over." I laughed again. "Though I gotta tell you, it's been pretty crazy here! But, yeah, I've been able to put things into context, and I'll take it. It's a good move."

"I'm very glad to hear it. When do you think you'll be back?"

"You know, I'd like to get started as soon as possible. People here aren't real welcoming, pretty hostile, actually. Be nice to see some of the guys again."

"Hostile? Why?"

"Oh, it's pretty crazy. You wouldn't believe it. I found a young girl murdered in a field the day I—"

I stopped because the line had been cut. They'd been listening in, as I knew they would. If they were stupid—real stupid—they believed my act and thought I was just an ordinary dude, and I was about to leave and get out of their hair. If they were smart and experienced, as I knew they were, they knew I had just sent a coded message asking for backup. The colonel would say I had been rash *and* stupid, that I had just signed my own death warrant. Now they would not let me off the island. They would hunt me down and kill me.

That was their plan, and I could hear Odin laughing in Valhalla.

The colonel would be wrong, as she so often was. Because in the first place, I had no intention of leaving the island. And as for being hunted down, I wanted them out in their droves, hunting me, because when the leopard gets behind his hunters, the hunters become the prey. And the more of them I killed before I went to the Company facilities, the better.

SEVEN

I STEPPED BACK INTO THE LOBBY. MARGUERITE WAS still writing in her ledger.

"The landline seems to have died too," I told her.

She looked up. "Yes, I know. Doctor Brown phoned while you were in the cubicle. She asked if you were here. I said you were, and she asked that you wait for her as she wants to see you. She'll be here at one. After that, the line went dead."

I thanked her and figured that if she'd called from a landline, she must have called from the Temple. Which meant Santa Maria, Olafsen, and the sheriff knew she'd called and had probably instructed her to do so.

I glanced at my watch. I had time to go to my room, strap on my Sig, and slip the Fairbairn and Sykes into my boot before a quick lunch. I told Marguerite, "I'll be down in fifteen minutes. I'll have a steak before I see the doc."

She nodded and headed for the kitchen as I headed for my room.

. . .

THE DOC PULLED up outside in a beaten-up red Toyota pickup at ten minutes past one. I didn't wait for her to come in. I pushed through the door and went over to lean on the truck with my hands and look down at her through the window.

"You wanted to see me. Here I am. If you're going to tell me to back off and leave the island, you're too late. I already told my boss I'm on my way back. I don't need this shit in my life anymore."

She let me finish, then said, "Get in."

I sighed elaborately, looking across the square at the Sea Breeze, with the fish going against the current. "I just got through telling you," I said without looking at her, but she cut me short.

"Get in, Harry."

I walked around to the passenger side, climbed in, and slammed the door.

"You sure you want to be seen with me? They might throw you out of the club."

"Shut up, Harry," she said, reversing out of the lot. "Do me a favor, and do yourself a favor, and shut up."

She accelerated past City Hall and down a narrow street with tall buildings on either side. A plaque said it was Middle Street. At the fourth turning on the left, she slowed abruptly and turned in. We rattled over some cobbles, past a back alley, and came out on a broad avenue framed with palm trees. On our side of the road, there were big, elegant colonial houses. On the far side, there was a paved promenade, and beyond that the white sand and the turquoise ocean. A sign said this was Beach Front Avenue.

She turned right, and we cruised along for a couple of hundred yards till we came to a sprawling clapboard house in need of paint and repairs. It had a wraparound veranda and was surrounded by lawn and big, old pine trees. She pulled in and parked outside a garage, killed the engine, and yanked on the handbrake.

"Get out, walk to the kitchen door at the back of the house, and try not to say anything smart."

I couldn't think of anything smart to say, so I got out, tried to keep in the cover of the trees, and made my way down an alley between the garage and the house till I came to the real lawn. It was overgrown with weeds, but there were a couple of stone steps that led up to the deck, where there was a door that looked like it gave onto a kitchen.

Behind me I heard the driver's door of the Toyota slam. I glanced and saw the doc making for the front door. I counted to sixty, and the kitchen door opened inward. She jerked her head toward the inside and said, "Come in."

"Gee, thanks. Are you going to be this friendly throughout our whole chat? Or do you plan to become a pain in the ass at some point?"

She didn't answer. She walked away, and I followed her through a door into a large room with a dining table at the near end. It stood by a French door that gave onto the overgrown lawn. At the other end of the room, there was a random scattering of slightly seedy armchairs and sofas, a coffee table with a half-empty bottle of Scotch on it, a glass, and an ashtray overflowing with stubs. The drapes were half drawn against the sunlight, and there was a faint smell of tobacco smoke on the air. It wasn't unpleasant.

She said, "Sit down," picked up the ashtray and the glass, and took them to the kitchen. I chose a chair where I wouldn't easily be seen from the avenue and sat. She came back a moment later with two glasses and an empty ashtray.

She set the glasses in front of me, and as she took a pack of Camels from the breast pocket of her shirt and lit up, she said, "Pour."

I poured, wondering how long my patience was going to last. I slid a glass across the table to her. She inhaled deeply and picked up the glass. As she blew out the smoke, she said, "What you did today was really stupid."

"Is that it? All this buildup for that?"

"You don't know who you're up against. They have decided to kill you."

"And they sent you to warn me?"

"You're wrong about that. I don't work for them any more than anyone else on this island does. If you live here, they own you, whether you like it or not. Cross them, the way you did today, and they simply eliminate you."

I studied her face a moment, then reached for my glass and said, "Yeah, well, they made me mad." I took a sip. "But I cooled down on my way back. There's fuck-all I can do here. You're in a state of anarchy. Neither Guyana nor Surinam wants to get involved, and they're probably being paid off by the Rat Labs anyway..." I shrugged. "It's not that they are above the law. Here, they *are* the law. I don't need that kind of problem, Doc. I'm getting out of here." Then, with an edge of bitterness, I added, "Is that what they sent you to do, scare me off?"

Her eyes were pretty bitter too. "Your holier than thou act is wearing thin, Harry. You're from the big, bad democratic republic where you all live in terror of the CIA and the NSA recording your conversations inviting Mom and Dad over for Christmas lunch. It's easy for you to be judgmental. Defiance for you is making a post on X and getting lots of outraged replies. Defiance on this island barely exists because it means, if you're lucky, getting badly beaten. I know. They bring them to me to patch up and get them fit for work again. If you're unlucky, your bloated body gets washed up on the shore a few days later. Nobody touches it. The sheriff collects it in his truck, and it gets cremated at the tanatorio. The House of Death."

I watched her deliver this, wondering how genuine the emotion was and how much that mattered. Implicit in what she was saying was that however much she didn't like it, she'd stab me in the back if they told her to. More likely still, it was an act, and she was here to both sound me out and scare me off.

I sighed laboriously and ran my fingers through my hair.

"I guess you're right. I'm sorry. Like I said, I've seen a lot of this shit, and I get upset."

"Yeah, but we are hotel managers, doctors, shopkeepers, women, children, and untrained men. We are not special ops killers. You make a noise and you can defend yourself, maybe. We make a noise, and we get silenced."

"I said I'm sorry." I spread my hands, still holding the drink, and shrugged. "So why'd you bring me here?"

She clasped her hands between her knees and looked down at her thumbs. After a moment, she said, "Because I thought... *hoped* you were going to do something."

"*Do* something? You just got through telling me I should do nothing. Now you're saying you hoped..." I trailed off, shaking my head. "Do something like what?"

"I don't know." She was still talking to her hands. "Something like bring it to the attention of the United Nations." Now she raised her face to fix me with her eyes. "Something like kill the bastards."

"Kill the bastards."

"Who's going to prosecute you? The sheriff is law enforcement because the mayor says so. The mayor is mayor because the sheriff says so. There is no law here—literally. There is no parliament, there is no legislature, there are no law books, statutes, courts, judges. There is no law on this island that says that killing a person is murder."

"This is something I never thought I'd see. A doctor asking me to kill a bunch of people."

"They are enslaving, raping, and killing people who cannot defend themselves. You were so indignant last night and this morning! What's happened to you? Surely Santa Maria didn't scare you!"

She'd said it to needle me, and it did. I told myself to be careful because this could be a subtle, skilled trap.

"Look, Doc, I have no ordnance here, I have no weapons, I have no men. Back in the day, maybe that wouldn't have been a problem, but I don't even know who I'm up against. I don't know who they are or how many of them there are. I was mad this morning because it looked like these guys were going to get away with what they were doing. And I guess they are. Because I have neither the means nor the information I would need to stop them."

She was watching her thumbs again. "I understand. But also you don't trust me because you think I am one of them."

"Of course I do. Wouldn't you?"

"I suppose so. But, Harry, there's a problem. They are not going to let you leave."

"What are you talking about?"

"Sheriff Scott told Mr. Santa Maria and Mr. Olafsen what you said to him. They decided you were a danger. They think you are connected to some organization that is spying on them. They are paranoid. So they cut the satellite connection—"

"They can do that?" I made it sound like I didn't believe it.

She gave a small, exasperated laugh, like she couldn't believe I didn't get it yet. "Of course they can. They can do anything they want. The dishes and the towers belong to the Company. They set them up, and they control them. They told me to phone and meet with you, and as soon as I was done, they cut the landlines too. They won't let you leave the island."

"How?"

"They'll be waiting for you at the port, the sheriff and his deputies, and men from the Company."

"So what was the point of sending you here? Why not simply—"

"You're not listening, Harry! You're not thinking! I am not supposed to be informing you and alerting you! I am supposed to be pumping you to find out who you are, who you work for, why the hell you're here! Instead of that, this slave of the cabal—this gutless traitor to her people, and her friends, and her *patients!*—is warning you of what they are doing and planning!"

I grunted a grunt that was more of a groan and leaned back in the chair with my eyes closed. I followed that up with a sigh, like she was getting to me.

"OK," I said, "I'm sorry. I guess you took a risk for me."

"Yes."

"Do you know who runs the Company?"

She gave a one-sided smile and a small laugh. "Yeah, he got bronchitis. They sent the sheriff to come and get me. Two hundred million dollars' worth of high-tech security and they drove me right through it."

"You told me they had medical facilities—"

"Uh-uh, *they* said they had medical facilities. What they have is some guy who probably failed his medical exams at the

University of Oolawanga, gives everyone antibiotics for everything, and if what they've got is serious, he passes them for extermination and replacement." She shook her head. "He wasn't going to let that butcher near him. The sheriff knows I'm a good doctor and..." She paused and trailed off.

I said, "What?"

"Mr. Drake called for me. The sheriff came and got me."

"Mr. Drake? He's an American?"

"I don't know. His accent is English, but that doesn't mean much. Mr. Drake is a strange man. He is unsettling to be with."

She took a deep breath and drained her glass, handing it to me to refill. I refilled both and handed hers back. She continued.

"Anyway, the point is, you will never get to Mr. Drake at the Company facility. It is too well guarded. It's like a military base. There must be dozens of well-armed men patrolling twenty-four hours a day, cameras on every inch of the place—"

I screwed up my face and shook my head. "*Why?* What the hell are they doing out there?"

"I don't know. I can only imagine it's something they are not allowed to do back home. They have deliberately conspired to keep this place outside any Western jurisdiction so they can carry on whatever they are doing there. But, Harry, that's not important right now. The thing you need to know is that Mr. Drake does not live on site."

I arched an eyebrow. "He doesn't? Where does he live?"

"At Sandy Cove. He has a big, luxurious, super modern mansion there."

"His security must be tight."

She shook her head. "You don't know this island. The security on the Company compound is impregnable. But the only crimes on this island are the ones committed by those bastards. The rest of the island is crime free. He has his alarm system, a butler who looks as though he eats bricks for breakfast, and a personal bodyguard. Aside from that there is nothing."

"But tonight..."

"Tonight he will have more security, unless we throw them off the scent."

"You shouldn't take that risk."

"Listen to me. His alarm system, all his electrical system, is connected to a generator in a kind of concrete shed in the woods at the back of his house. If you disable that, his alarm system and all his electric locking devices will fail."

"How do you know this?"

"I told you he had serious bronchitis. The first time I saw him was at the Company compound. I sent him home, and I saw him several times at his house. He's a pain in the ass, and he told me all about the amazing electronics in his house. Now stop interrupting. I have a sailing boat on the beach here, a little farther down. You knock me out, tie me up, steal the boat, and head out as though you were headed for Georgetown, but two or three miles out, you turn west and circle around the Moles to come into the cove from the north."

I thought about it. It wasn't bad. I wondered for a moment if I had misjudged her.

"They'll be mad at you. You have to offer them something in mitigation. You managed to get something out of me before I got mad and jumped you."

She frowned. "Like what?"

"Tell them I'm CIA."

"Are you?"

"No, but tell them I told you I was, and that Central Intelligence is investigating satellite photographs that suggest there might be a lithium mine out there, and they want to know who's running it."

She narrowed her eyes at me for a long moment. We talked for another fifteen or twenty minutes. Then, without warning, I knocked her unconscious, settled her comfortably on her bed, tied and gagged her, and left the house. I took the keys to her Toyota and drove back to my hotel.

EIGHT

HER SAILING BOAT WAS THE *ENDURING HOPE*, A thirty-foot cutter anchored maybe a hundred yards off the shore. I jumped the low wall from the promenade onto the sand with a rucksack on my back. I trudged down through the fishing boats to where the small, transparent waves were lapping at the white sand and sat. I pulled off my boots, hung them around my neck, and waded out into the ocean. It was an easy swim, and in a couple of minutes, I was clambering aboard the small yacht. Five minutes after that, I was headed south out of the broad Es Arenal bay.

I had to head south for a mile just in case what the doc had been telling me was true. By the time I'd put her out, she had me half-convinced that she was genuine. The other half of me was pretty much convinced that she was a clever, subtle woman who was trying to wind me around her little finger. Whichever was true, I had to minimize my risks. So anyone watching me leave Es Arenal should see me headed south, as though I was heading for Georgetown. At three miles, I'd be below the horizon and lost to sight. There I would turn west and circle around the Mole and North Mole to ease into Sandy Cove. Averaging six knots for the first mile, then easing to four or five, it was going to take me all of three or four hours. That would get me there shortly before sunset.

Night falls fast at the equator. One minute it's sunset, the next it's night, and that tends to happen around six p.m. My aim was to get there at about five-thirty and drop anchor at the North Mole headland, out of sight of the cove. Then take the inflatable dinghy and row ashore under cover of darkness.

It was a strangely peaceful journey. The sun was declining in the west, there was a good breeze out of the northeast, and the sea had only a slight swell. So I was able to sit at the helm smacking over the small waves under the sun, with just enough salt spray to keep me awake but also stop me from thinking too deeply. The questions I had were questions I could not answer until I had Drake talking to me. So I put it all into the back of my mind and enjoyed the freedom of the wind and the ocean.

I got there on schedule as the sun was approaching the horizon and the western sky was a blaze of red and yellow, broken up by streaks of violet clouds. I dropped the sales and the anchor at the headland, as close to the cliffs as I dared, and waited for darkness to fall.

I didn't have to wait long. At six, the sun hit the horizon, the sky caught fire, and in less than a minute, it went dark. There was no moon. By starlight I lowered the dinghy into the sea, climbed in, and released the rope. A minute later, I was approaching the end of the headland, where it turned in to Sandy Cove. There I paused to look over my shoulder. Over on the left of the cove, I could see an extended cluster of lights. This was what the doc had told me was like a resort with bars, restaurants, and even a nightclub, where the management from the Company came to let off steam. Normal islanders were not served, only the directors and the management from the Company.

The area I assumed was the sandy beach she had told me about was dark, but over on the right, I could see a much smaller cluster of lights, which, according to the doc, would be Drake's house. I lined it up and started pulling on the oars, keeping as close to the right side of the cove as I dared, getting ever closer to the rhythmic sigh of the beach.

After about five minutes, the surf was carrying me in to the shore. I guided the dinghy in to where the sand met the cliff and the woodland, jumped out, and pulled the dinghy into the cover of the boulders and the pines. There I hunkered down and waited in silence, listening to every sound around me. There was the background throb and laughter of the bars and restaurants across the bay. There was the rhythmic thud and sigh of the small waves as they hit the sand and then withdrew, and behind me and to my right, there were the muffled, secret sounds of a forest at night. Nowhere did I hear men moving, men alerted to the dinghy and coming to inspect.

After a couple of minutes, I rose and moved silently in among the trees, heading up toward the lights of Drake's villa. More than a villa, it was an ultra-modern mansion made of huge, whitewashed cubes and great sheets of plate glass. I came to within a hundred yards of the great sprawl of cubes. Any closer and I would have to break cover. I lay behind a cluster of ferns and watched the house for about half an hour.

Through the glass, in the glow of the rooms, I could see figures. On the ground floor there was a man seated in a large armchair. Outside that room, there was a guy seated near an illuminated pool. In the glow from the pool and a couple of lamps in the trees, I could see he had an assault rifle across his knees. At one point, a silhouette entered the living room and seemed to deliver a glass and a bottle to the seated figure, then left.

Eventually I withdrew back into the woodland and moved around to the front of the house. Here the road wound out of the downs, and on the bend where it turned into the complex of bars and restaurants, a short drive led into the grounds of Drake's mansion. The drive was flanked by tropical gardens where flowering trees I couldn't identify surrounded fountains that were more like large ponds where water flowed over rocks to splash into the pools. The garden area was contained within a low wall. Beside the door, there were two guys sitting quietly in a couple of white plastic garden chairs, each with a rifle in his lap.

I withdrew again, back among the sand, the brown pine needles, and the tall trees. It took me about fifteen minutes, but pretty soon I found the electric generator the doc had told me about. I opened my rucksack and took out the suppressor Andy had included in my Gladstone bag, fitted it to my Sig, and blew off the padlock. I took out a couple more things he'd included for me, made some adjustments, and headed back to Drake's house.

As I went, I took the Fairbairn and Sykes from my boot and held it upside-down with the blade concealed behind my forearm. I came to a point where the trees fringed the road and stepped out, then made my way back down toward the villa, in full view.

The two guys took no notice of me. That told me they were used to visitors of the resort wandering past. As I approached the gate, I raised my left hand in a salute.

"Hey!" I smiled so they could see my teeth. "My Jeep broke down!" As I said it, I opened the gate and stepped inside. They got to their feet. I kept walking like they weren't holding rifles. "Can I use your phone? I left mine at the villa—"

They were moving toward me. One had his right hand raised, palm out to stop me.

"I'm sorry, sir, you can't come in here. You have to go back."

In a fraction of a second, my mind registered that if Drake and the doc had set me up, these guys would not be so relaxed. They would have been expecting me, beaten me to the ground, or even killed me.

I keep the Fairbairn and Sykes more than razor sharp. I frowned at his hand like I was startled and expostulated, "Whoa! What's that on your arm?" As I said it, I flashed my right hand out and severed his radial and ulnar arteries and veins, as well as his tendons. In the same movement, I stepped forward and smashed my instep into the other guy's balls, and as my foot touched the ground, I slammed the knife back into the side of the first guy's neck and wrenched it out the front of his throat.

Guy number two was on his knees, wheezing and weeping. I hunkered down in front of him. Behind me, I heard the soft thud of his pal hitting the ground.

"How many inside?"

He stared into my face. It was painful and pathetic. I repeated, "How many?"

He said, "One at the pool, in back. One in house."

I drove the knife down behind his left collarbone, severing arteries and plunging deep into his heart. He went into spasm for a second, then went to hell.

I had no idea if they had CCTV or any other security. One thing was clear: I had no time to waste. I sprinted for the front door. I knew if I knocked or rang, unless I had been seen on

CCTV, the bodyguard inside would open. The chances were good. I figured if I'd been seen on CCTV, I'd already be making like a colander.

I reached the door. The was a button on the right. I rang. After fifteen seconds, I heard movement, and the door opened. He was six foot two and probably from Samoa, where they use their bare hands to quarry granite. I stuck my left index finger an inch from his nose and said, "Wait!"

He got as far as sneering and reaching for it before I drove the fighting knife through his solar plexus. It's a cruel way to kill someone because they lose the use of their lungs, and they suffocate instead of bleeding out. But it meant he couldn't shout or raise the alarm. As he doubled up, struggling for air his diaphragm couldn't draw in, I removed the knife and rammed it into the side of his neck. Then he didn't need air anymore.

I lowered his three hundred pounds of dead weight to the floor with difficulty and eased the door closed with my foot. I shoved the knife back in my boot and slipped the rucksack off my shoulder. I took out a plastic grocery bag with about two pounds of groceries in it and dropped it on Mega-Man's belly. Then I pulled the Sig from my waistband.

Ahead of me, there were two arches, one to my right and one to my left. I made for the right arch because I knew it had to lead to the pool and the living room where I had seen the guy in the chair receiving his drink.

I came right away to a darkened dining area. Through the glass, I could see lawn and trees and the glow of the pool to the right. At the end of the room, there was another arch, through which light was glowing. I took four strides and saw the shape of the guy through the glass. He had his back to me. I double-tapped. The first slug sent fine spider webs through the inch-thick glass. The second punched through the glass and the back of his skull. I turned.

Across the room, there was a man in his late forties or early fifties. His hair was very black and exquisitely cut. His clothes were elegant and looked very expensive. He was watching me with no apparent emotion.

"That glass," he said. His accent was New England, but Boston Brahmin rather than Townie. I frowned at the statement, momentarily taken aback. He had a black hardback book in his hand, and he closed it to point at the shattered window. "The glass is worth more than the man you shot through it." He set the book on the table beside him and gave a small shrug with his shoulders and his eyebrows. "That pane of glass is worth more than all four men you killed to get in here." He smiled. "And by the looks of it, more useful too."

"You're Drake."

"Thank you. How much do I weigh?"

"It's good you have a sense of humor. You're going to need it."

He gave a small snort. "No doubt, but I think that applies to us both, Mr. Bauer."

"What are you doing at the compound, what the islanders call the Company?"

"And if I don't tell you, you'll torture me to make me talk. Before you do that, Mr. Bauer, you should give some thought to how you're going to get out of here."

"Yeah? How's that?"

His smile wasn't so much thin as anorexic. "The whole place is locked down. You can't get out, and as we speak, a dozen of my men are surrounding the house. You are well and truly royally fucked."

"Is it a lithium mine?"

He closed his eyes and laughed. It was tolerant and patronizing and made me want to go over and spread his face all over the wall.

"Yes," he said, and opened his eyes. "Yes, it's a lithium mine. It is also a processing plant and a laboratory where we work with nanotechnologies you could not even begin to understand."

"But you're a defense contractor. So you're making weapons for the US military."

He closed his eyes again, but this time he sighed, like he was getting bored wasting his time talking to a moron. "How can I talk to you, Harry? You are so ignorant, you are so far removed from the reality of this world, you are so out of touch with the forces that control you and your world." He sat forward to stare at me. "This US military that you talk about, what is it?"

"What are you talking about?"

"*What is it?* A bunch of weapons, a bunch of men and women, a handful of generals who think they run it. You ask me, do we make weapons for them? No, Harry, we don't make weapons *for* them. *They* make war for *us*."

"Who is 'us'?"

He mixed a long "Ooooh" with a laugh and ended up with, "I think you know the answer to that, Harry. You know who we are, and we know who you are. We are the Eye in the pyramid, we are the apex, the center of earthly power. We control the violence, and that means we control everything."

"I've heard that before. Is that how it works? Violence is the most valuable commodity on Earth. He who controls the violence and is willing to use it is the most powerful man on Earth."

"Yes, Harry, that's how it works. So let me tell you what happens next. You set down your weapons, we have a meaningful exchange in which you tell me all about Cobra and Brigadier 'Buddy' Byrd, and when we are done with our full and frank discussion, my men will come in, and depending on how willing you are to cooperate, we will decide what to do with you."

I was frowning because I was curious. "You let your men in *after* we talk? What makes you think I am going to tell you a goddamn thing if your men are not putting electrodes on my balls?"

He raised his shoulders a quarter of an inch. "You know that if you don't cooperate, they will do a lot more than use electrodes. They will skin you alive limb by limb and take your eyes out. It will be pain and horror beyond your wildest nightmares."

"And you don't want them to be privy to what I tell you."

"Precisely."

"Skin me alive, limb by limb, and take out my eyes."

"And you know I am serious."

I nodded. "I do." I still had the Sig in my hand. "You'll want my cell as well as my gun and my knife," I said and reached in my back pocket. I held up the cell for him to see, and as I did so, I pressed the right-hand side button.

NINE

There was a violent explosion outside, and instantly the lights went out.

I had calculated the distance in my mind while he was talking, and I stepped over to him and delivered a vicious right hook with the butt of the Sig. He gasped, sagged forward, and doubled up in his chair, keening.

"We'll catch up, Drake," I told him. "We'll have this conversation again, in a better setting."

Outside I could hear men shouting and running. I heard the front door open and pressed the button on my phone twice. The plastic grocery bag containing two pounds of C4 exploded in the face of the men who were bursting through the door.

I moved quickly with the suppressed Sig held out in front of me. Even in the dark, the entrance was a grotesque scene of carnage, dismembered limbs, and gore. There was an intense smell of metallic marzipan mixed with the stench of burned human flesh. It was impossible to count accurately, but I estimated the remains of four men inside the door.

Outside there was one badly damaged man lying on the lawn. He was making noises, so I shot him in the head to put him out of his misery. There were two more men. One was standing unsteadily with his hands covering his face and moaning. Another was behind him, on his knees on the grass. He had his eyes closed and his hands over his ears. He was groaning. I shot them both in the head, vaulted the wall, and ran into the woods.

As I ran through the deep sand, I thought. He'd said there were twelve men surrounding the house, waiting to move in when he gave them the OK. I had killed maybe seven or eight of those twelve. If he'd been telling the truth, which was a big if, that left maybe four or five. At least one would stay with him to get medical help; that meant four would be on my tail. And as I left the darkened house behind me, heading toward the beach and the dinghy, I saw them.

They were standing around the dinghy. Two were looking toward me but couldn't see me among the trees. Another was searching the beach with a powerful flashlight. The fourth methodically put four rounds into the boat, and it began to deflate. I turned and ran. I had no clear idea in my head of what my plan was. At its most basic, it was get to the Company compound, gather evidence of how it was being used, destroy it, interrogate Drake, kill him and as much of the management as I could, and get off I-Takka in one piece. All with a Sig P226, a Fairbairn and Sykes fighting knife, and the few 'goodies' supplied by Andy and the British Embassy. The plan wasn't ambitious. It was impossible.

Pretty soon the sand underfoot gave way to firmer earth, and I was able to pick up speed. I could hear shouts behind me and the roar of engines. When I looked over my shoulder, I could see cars pulling up outside Drake's house, and I knew pretty soon Sheriff Jeremiah Scott would be on his way. I also knew that the four men I'd seen on the beach would be after me in trucks, and I had to lose them.

My first thought as I ran was that they would expect me to head east, toward Es Arenal, the hotel, my car and, most important of all, the port. For that I would have to cross the road and head into the downs—and risk getting caught in the headlights of any one of the trucks and cars that were revving up at the resort around Drake's house. But if I turned right, where the forest grew thicker, I would head into the Pine Valley between the Mole and North Mole. If they didn't follow me, I had the choice of heading back to North Mole and climbing down to the yacht or making my way to the Cala and from there heading northeast into the downs toward the Company compound.

If they did follow me, the untamed forest would give me the opportunity to turn the tables and become hunter instead of prey.

Instinctively, giving it no thought, I turned right and ran fast into the impenetrable darkness, dodging trees but crashing through branches, taking care only to protect my eyes but giving no regard to how clear my trail was. On the contrary, at this stage I wanted the trail to be clear and easy to follow, even in the dark. Let them think I was panicking. Let them feel confident that that they had me.

About a quarter of a mile in, the valley seemed to narrow to a broad canyon, and the sides began to climb steeply, looking black against the translucent, star-peppered sky. Here I stopped and looked back. Anyone with the slightest skill in hunting would be able to follow the track I had left, even at night. And even as I told myself that, through the dense foliage and the reeds that swarmed several feet high among the base of the trees, I saw the dim glow of flashlights bobbing up and down.

I turned back and scanned the forest ahead of me on both sides. Up to my left, on the steep slope of the Mole, about a hundred yards up, I could make out the slight luminescence of large, pale boulders.

I moved swiftly, but this time I made no noise and left no tracks until I was closing on the rocks. Then I paused and trampled a couple of ferns, broke some twigs on a bush, and for good measure put my rucksack where it was just visible from fifteen or twenty feet away. Then I moved back the way I'd come a few yards, moved in among the trees, and lay on my belly to wait.

The smell of pine resin was intense. I closed my eyes and listened. There are a thousand small noises in a forest at night which, unless you listen for them, you will never hear. But above them all was the crash and the trample of four men breaking their way through the bushes and the trees and trampling the ferns. They were close, and soon I heard them maybe ten yards beneath me at the bottom of the canyon. I made my breathing shallow and remained motionless and silent. A voice came to me.

"What happened? Where is he?"

He was answered by a voice that sounded Australian or Kiwi. "Did the fuckin' aliens come down and take him?"

A third voice, older and deeper. "He stopped running and is hidden up there somewhere. I bet he's no more than thirty or forty yards away. Get back. Get some cover."

I heard movement, rustling, the cracking of twigs, whispered voices. The older voice said, "Up there."

The Kiwi whispered, "That's where I'd go."

The first voice said, "Go on, then."

"Cover me."

There was more rustling, then the careful but clumsy movement of a body through the undergrowth, moving up the steep slope. The rustling grew close, and suddenly a figure appeared barely six or seven feet from me. I didn't breathe until he'd passed and was moving toward the rocks with his back to me. He froze suddenly and dropped to his haunches. I saw him look down the slope. A flashlight played over him, and he shaded his eyes with one hand and jabbed his finger at the rocks with the other. He'd seen the edge of the rucksack.

The light shifted to the rock, casting long black shadows across he hill, and the guy moved slowly and carefully closer. There was a tree on his right which would obscure the view from below. He moved behind it, and I squeezed the trigger. There was a *phut!* His head whiplashed, and his brain exploded out of his face. He slumped forward and lay in a crumpled heap, out of sight. Below they might have heard the *phut!* from the Sig, but they would not have seen the flash from the muzzle. They had no reason to think the shot had come from anywhere other than the rocks until they saw the exit wound. I had several seconds in which to move.

I used them to change my position to twelve or fifteen feet farther down the hill. There I could no longer see the corpse or the rocks, which were both concealed by the tall pine, but when the three remaining men climbed the hill toward the rocks, I would be very close behind them.

I remained motionless lying at the base of a large pine and kept my breathing slow and shallow. I heard rustling and grunting and saw the circle of light dancing and swinging up the hill. The deeper voice, which I was beginning to recognize, muttered, "Turn that damn flashlight off. You might as well put a goddamn target on your head."

The light disappeared, and a second voice breathed, "Can't see a damned thing!"

Then Rishi's unmistakable sing-song. "Stop complaining. You should go ahead and have a look, we'll cover you."

And the deeper voice I was now sure was the sheriff: "Yeah, go on ahead, Jack. We'll keep you covered. If he raises his head, we'll blow it off."

"Great! Why me? Why can't Rishi go?"

"Just do what I'm tellin' you. We've got your back."

One set of steps got louder and faster as the guy started climbing ahead. He passed within a few feet of me, and a moment later, I saw the large form of the sheriff and Rishi just behind him. I waited till Rishi was nine or ten feet from me and the other guy was coming to the bend. He stopped when he saw the Kiwi's body, and I got a clean shot right through his temple. I didn't pause. I only had to drop the sights a couple of inches and squeeze the trigger and I blew Rishi's brains all over the sheriff's face as he turned.

Having somebody's brains blown all over your face can have a momentarily paralyzing effect. It gave me a couple of seconds to get to my feet move around a tree and approach the sheriff from behind. He was walking in small circles, wiping his face and going, "Ah! Ah! Oh...! Lord!"

A sudden rage possessed me as I came within reach. I grabbed a fistful of his collar from behind and drove a savage hook into his floating ribs and his liver. He didn't shout because the pain was so intense he couldn't breathe. I threw him to the ground and knelt on the back of his neck with my left knee and placed the muzzle of the Sig on the back of his thigh.

"When you need to convince people to talk, Sheriff, sometimes you have to prove to them that you're serious. But I am telling you I am a ruthless son of a bitch. Do you believe me? Or do I have to prove it to you?"

He was weeping and babbling into the dirt, but I could hear him saying, "No! No! No!"

"I'm going to ask you some questions, Jeremiah, and you are going to answer quick and clear, no hesitation, no thinking. You understand me. If I think you're lying, I'll put a hole through your knee and leave you here to die."

I stood and told him, "Sit up."

He struggled into a sitting position with his back against the trunk of a pine. I hunkered down in front of him and aimed the Sig at his left knee.

"Who killed Maisy Middleton?"

His face seemed to crumple in on itself, and his bottom lip curled in on itself. He shook his head, "I swear, Mr. Bauer. I swear I don't know."

"Who does know?"

"Mr. Drake. He's the only one who knows."

"Is it him? Did he kill her?"

"No. It's somebody else. But he knows who."

"You're doing good. Keep it up and you might just get out of this alive. How does Joseph Santa Maria, the governor, fit into this?"

He gave a small frown. "The girls? He has nothing to do with that. He's part of the Company. He has the political connections. He deals with Guyana and Surinam."

"The Company is bribing their governments—"

"Their presidents, yeah. I don't know how much, but they get big payoffs."

"What exactly does the Company do?"

"Most of it is classified. I know they're mining for lithium, and they process it. But they have labs there. I've only been a couple of times. They do top secret defense stuff. That's all I know. I'm telling the truth."

"Tell me about the workers."

"They took three hundred islanders. They weren't on any official census or record, except here on the island. So nobody was going to miss them. They made them an offer where they said they were going to pay them way above going rates here, plus they could bring their families, live in beautiful housing onsite. They wanted the whole family to go so they could get them all working but also to reduce the risk of anyone coming looking for their parents or kids, or brothers and sisters."

"And they use them as slaves."

He swallowed. "Yeah." He hesitated a moment, watching me. "But not just as slaves. They have them working in the mine, but they also use some of them for experiments."I could feel the hot coal of rage in my belly building. I asked quietly, "What kind of experiments?"

"I don't know. Like I said, those things are classified. But every so often, they choose a couple of people and take them away. Nobody ever sees them again. Sometimes it's men, sometimes it's women or kids. I asked the governor. He said they use them for experiments, but he wouldn't tell me what kind."

"What about the mayor and the priest? What's their part in all this?"

"Nothing. The mayor is just a front to give the Company legitimacy. Father da Silva is pretty much the same. I've told you all I know, Mr. Bauer. I've cooperated with you. What are you going to do?"

"Kill you."

I shot him in the head and made my way back down into the canyon.

TEN

PROGRESS WAS SLOW AND LABORIOUS. THE FOREST on the Mole was ancient and dense, particularly on the east side, as I approached the Cala bay. The forest floor was a sea of ferns growing up to five feet in height, and the trees were so densely packed at times it was impossible to move through them, and I had to make wide detours. But eventually I came to a narrow track which led out of the trees to a high cliff that overlooked the bay below. There was still no moon, but in the starlight, I could make out the hulking yet ghostly shape of the satellite dish across the bay, and beyond it, close to the pulsing fan from the lighthouse, the Temple, where a limpid glow emerged from the door and the windows.

I checked my watch. It was eleven-thirty. It wasn't Sunday, and it wasn't Christmas. That made me wonder why they had lights on and the door open in the middle of the night. Maybe their god was available twenty-four-seven, not just on weekends.

Or maybe it was something else.

From that point on, the trek became easier. As I walked

along the cliff edge, I had a good view of most of the island, and I was able to see all the traffic that moved along its two roads. There was a lot less than I expected, but I did see a convoy of three sets of headlights move into Es Arenal, and half an hour after that, as I was descending toward the Cala, I watched what I assumed to be the same headlights leave and head back toward the crossroads. After that, my descent toward the cove brought me below the tree line, and I lost sight of the roads.

What I also saw, and it held my attention, was a subdued dome of radiance at the far side of I-Takka, near North Faro, that part of the island I hadn't visited yet. The glow had to be from the Company. It wasn't their god who was working twenty-four-seven. It was their masters. Whether the headlights moved in the direction of the glow I didn't get to see, but I had a pretty strong hunch they would eventually.

It took me another hour to reach the cove. For a moment, I was tempted to follow it around and find out what was going down at the church. Maybe I should have done that, but I was driven by a more pressing need and a growing sense of urgency which I was finding hard to ignore. So instead of continuing around the Cala and heading for the Temple on South Faro, I kept going pretty much straight in a northeasterly direction, toward the crossroads.

By the time I reached the blacktop, it was past two a.m., and I was beginning to feel exhausted. I had misread the lay of the land coming out of the forest and added another two miles to my walk. Now I was about two miles from Es Arenal and just a quarter of a mile from the crossroads itself.

My plan, such as it was, was to collect my stuff from the hotel and find somewhere where I could sleep and rest and have something to eat. I was aware that staying any longer at the hotel could put Marguerite and Camilla at risk. So it was time to move on. Somewhere in the back of my mind, I also had the thought that I should check on the doc, or at least alert someone to the fact that she needed to be untied. I was ninety percent sure that she was cooperating with the Company and had set me up. So they probably already knew where she was and in what condition. But there was ten percent of me that was willing to believe she was acting under duress and wanted to help me if she could.

I stepped onto the blacktop and headed south toward Es Arenal, but I had only taken a few steps when I saw a blob of light emerge from the village. It shone very brightly, then seemed to morph and separate into two as it drew closer.

I knew I'd been seen, but I moved off the road and hunkered down among the low bushes and rocks that bordered the road. It was only one car, and I figured if it was an islander he'd make like he hadn't seen me and drive on by, but if it was men from the Company, I could take them and use their car.

It slowed and came to a halt twelve or fifteen feet from me. All I could see was the glow from the headlights on full beam and the vague outline of a Jeep or a Range Rover. I could hear the quiet rumble of the engine, and then the soft whine of the window coming down. I lined up the door and waited. It didn't open, but I heard the hiss of a woman's voice calling in a whisper, "*Harry? Harry, is that you?*"

I knew the voice. It was Camilla. I kept her lined up and said, "Kill the lights."

There was a moment's hesitation. Then she killed them, and I took my time staring through the windows, allowing my eyes to adjust. She seemed to be alone, and as though to confirm it, she said, "*It's me, Camilla. I'm alone. I was looking for you!*"

I approached the vehicle from the back, peered in through the back windows, then climbed in the passenger seat and slammed the door. She was staring at me, frowning. I said, "What the hell are you doing out here?"

"I was looking for you. What happened?"

"Let's get back to the hotel. You shouldn't be out here tonight."

"Why? What's happened, Harry? Mom—"

She stopped, put the truck in gear, and turned it around.

"What about your mother?"

"They came. They beat her and threatened to kill her."

Her voice wavered and became a little shrill at the end. But she bit back the tears and got a grip.

"What did they want?" I asked, but I already knew the answer.

"They wanted you."

We entered the town. It was dead, dark, and silent. She pulled up outside the hotel and killed the engine.

"They thought she knew where you were."

My mind was racing. They knew where I'd gone because they had been expecting me. It was the very reason I didn't trust the doc. But this was different. They were locking down the island and hunting me because of what I had done to Drake and his men. And I had stupidly put Marguerite and Camilla at risk.

"I need you to listen very carefully, Camilla. I am going to collect some things from my room. Then I am going to leave. I am going to steal a boat and sail to Guyana. You understand?" She nodded, still frowning. "As soon as I am gone, you call them on the landline, can you do that?"

"No, I won't do it."

"Listen to me. You give me ten minutes, that's all I need.

Then you call them and you tell them what I have told you. I threatened you and forced you to tell me where I could get a boat. What did you tell me?"

She was blinking back tears. "The Marina. It's down on the beach, about a quarter of a mile away, going east along the shore."

"OK, you tell them that and they won't trouble you anymore."

Her face dissolved, and she started to cry. "But can't you stay and help us? Mom is badly beaten. It's really bad here, Harry. You don't realize..."

She trailed off. I looked deep into her eyes.

"You tell them what I told you. When they go to the marina, I will have taken a boat. But it is best you don't know what I am going to do. You understand? I asked you where I can steal a boat, and you told me."

"They said the sheriff disappeared and they think you killed him. Is that true?"

"The sheriff and his deputies won't be covering for any more child killers. The less you know the better."

She reached out and touched my hand. "Will you come and see Mom? She didn't tell them anything about you."

"How bad is she?"

The light from the street lamps outside cast a diagonal shadow across her face. Her lip curled in, and tears slid down her cheek. "She's bad," she said in a half whisper.

"OK, let's go."

She unlocked the door, and when we were inside, she locked it again, and we climbed the stairs to the bedrooms. She led me to the end of the corridor, paused outside a door, and knocked. After a pause, she opened it and spoke into the shadows.

"Mom, Mr. Bauer is here. He wants to see you."

I went in, and she turned her face away. She tried to speak but was overcome with sobbing. Her face was swollen, and in the dim light from the corridor outside, I could see huge blue bruises. Her left eye was closed, and there were knuckle marks visible where she had been punched.

"Did they strike the body or just the face?"

Camilla frowned at me. I met her eye and repeated the question.

"It was mainly the face, but they hit her on the back and the belly as well. They kicked her when she was on the floor."

I held out my hand. "Give me the keys to the truck. Lock me out. I'll be back in ten minutes. Fifteen at the most."

"Where are you going?"

"She needs a doctor."

She hesitated. "Doctor Brown… She's one of them."

"Not any more," I snarled. "There is no them. They just don't know it yet."

I threw my rucksack on my bed and clattered down the stairs with Camilla behind me. I went out and heard the door click and lock. I kept the headlights off and drove at speed down to the sea and onto Beach Front Avenue. As I accelerated toward Doc Brown's house, I could see a dim light showing through her drapes. I stopped outside, made her deck and her front door in four strides, and put a 9mm slug through her lock. Then I kicked in the door.

She was sitting on the sofa with a glass of whiskey in her hand and a cigarette in her mouth. The cigarette dropped when she gaped at me. I didn't pause. Two more strides took me up beside her. I grabbed her by the back of her collar and dragged her to her feet.

"Get up!"

"Harry, I didn't—"

"Shut up!"

I dragged her across the floor, stumbling and half running. Her glass and the bottle fell to the floor. "Get your medical bag! Now!"

She stared at me a moment, then grabbed an old, black leather bag from beside the sofa. I took her arm and dragged her out across the deck and shoved her in the passenger seat. She kept repeating, "Harry! Wait! *Harry!*"

I slammed the door and went to the driver's side. I got behind the wheel, and she said it again. "Harry, you have to listen to me—"

I scowled at her and said quietly, "Shut up. Don't talk."

I made a U-turn and headed back toward the hotel.

"Marguerite has been beaten and kicked to a pulp. She needs medical care, and you are the closest thing to a doctor on this godforsaken island. You will heal her, and she will make a full recovery."

I was silent while I negotiated a couple of bends. When I had pulled up outside the hotel again, I turned to face her. "I don't know exactly how many men I killed tonight. Somewhere between twelve and fourteen, including Sheriff Jeremiah Scott. If anything happens to Marguerite or Camilla, believe me, Caroline, you will be joining them in hell."

"Judge, jury, and executioner."

"Yeah. Remember that."

"It's so bloody easy for you. But what is a woman supposed to do against those thugs? You don't understand what goes on on this island. They do awful things to you if you don't toe the line."

"Get out."

I swung down, grabbed the doc, and shoved her toward the

hotel entrance. Camilla must have been watching for me because the door opened, and I shoved Caroline inside. "Upstairs."

Camilla led the way, and I followed behind Caroline. Camilla paused at the door, stared at Caroline a moment without speaking, then opened it, and Caroline went in. She stood frozen in the middle of the floor. Camilla moved past her and switched on the bedside lamp. Marguerite winced for a moment but held the doctor's eye.

I said, "I have to go out, but I'll be back. I'm telling you, Doc, you had better make damn sure nothing happens to her while I'm gone."

She seemed not to hear me. She sat on the bed, took Marguerite's hand, and began quietly to weep.

I turned and left.

In my room, I dumped the remaining contents of the rucksack on the bed. There was a Tavor X95 bullpup with three thirty round magazines. There were a couple of boxes of ammo for the Sig, ten cakes of C4 with detonators, and that was about it. To say it was not up to the job in hand was the understatement of the century. I had just about enough ordnance to blow a hole in the gate and get shot. It crossed my mind to abort the plan, but there was no turning back now. This was not just a fight to execute the enemy anymore. This was a fight for survival, for all of us. I had to go ahead, and I had to win.

I heard the door open behind me. It was Camilla. She closed the door and stood staring at the stuff on the bed.

"You shouldn't see this," I said.

"You're going to take on all of them, alone, with that."

"I have a plan."

"We're going to die, aren't we?"

"It's possible."

“I don’t want to die, Harry.”

“I am going to do everything I can to stop that from happening. They’re going to come after me, Camilla. And they’ll know exactly where I am.”

“Will you hold me, please?”

I put my arms around her, and she clung to me. After a moment, she raised her face to mine. I knew it was wrong, but I also knew death was right there in the room with us, and that the chances of any of us surviving that night were practically nonexistent. I took her mouth with mine, and we kissed hungrily. Then we fell on the bed, among the instruments of death, and made love.

ELEVEN

Dawn was turning the eastern horizon gray. The road was long and straight and narrow. In the distance, I could see the lighthouse: a narrow, shapely silhouette against the paling horizon.

Blocking my path were two Land Rovers with their headlights on full beam and racks on their roofs. They were maybe a hundred yards away, and if they'd wanted to, they could have riddled me with bullets already several times over. But I knew they didn't want that—not yet. Before they killed me, they wanted to know who was behind me.

It was hard to make out how many men there were. I figured eight, four in each truck. But their silhouettes warped, twisted, and blended as they moved in the intense lights. One figure moved forward. He shouted through a bullhorn.

"*Put down your weapons and put your hands in the air!*"

I climbed out of the cab of the Jeep with my hands in the air. "*I'm not armed! I've come to talk to Drake and Santa Maria. I want to make a deal.*"

There was some movement and murmured voices. Then three men in grunt uniforms moved toward me. I noticed as they approached that they were carrying Sig Sauer M7 rifles. These were next generation weapons, only then in the process of replacing the M4 under the NGSW program. If they wanted to know who I was, I was pretty anxious to know who they were too.

Two of them kept me covered while the third made a thorough and professional search. When he was done, he searched inside the vehicle. He gave the thumbs up to the men watching him and turned to me.

"Follow us in your vehicle, sir. You'll follow the lead car, and the second car will follow you. I am instructed to tell you that any attempt to deviate from the route set by the lead car will result in your vehicle coming under sustained fire. Do you understand, sir?"

"I understand, soldier."

I climbed back in the Jeep and approached the two Land Rovers. The one on my left reversed off the road, while the one on my right took the lead. I noticed, as I passed it, that the one on my left was an adapted flatbed with a powerful machine gun mounted in the back. If I deviated from the course set by the lead car, they would have to collect what was left of me with a mop.

We turned left off the blacktop about a mile from the lighthouse and followed a broad dirt track through rocks and twisted shrubs to a large complex on the western side of the cliff. It was surrounded by a fifteen foot steel wall, reminiscent of the one separating Mexico from the United States. Surrounding the wall were three consecutive rows of razor wire covering a depth of maybe fifteen feet, and spotlights and machine guns were mounted on every inch. If Drake had not been worried about home invasions, his Company was not taking any chances.

The big, steel gate rolled back, and we drove into an area maybe twenty-five feet long and twelve or fifteen feet across. Ahead of us there was another steel gate, and when the one behind us closed, we were essentially in a steel well, with four heavy machine guns pointed down at us. From the lights that winked on and off on the walls above us, I gathered they were using sensors of various types to scan my vehicle. Apparently they were satisfied because the gate ahead opened, and we rolled through.

As we moved into the complex, I became aware for the first time of its size. In the growing light of the early morning, I saw, on our left, the huge mine that had been dug out of the cliff in massive, descending steps.

On our right we passed what looked like a barracks. After that was a second barracks, but this one was surrounded by a barbed wire fence, and guard towers stood at each corner, giving it the look and feel of a concentration camp, though I could not see any inmates in there. I already had it clear in my mind, but as we drove past those rows of shacks, I knew, with no shadow of a doubt, that they would never let me leave that place alive.

We came then to a broad, open space beyond which there were several buildings set in a long row. They looked like prefabricated modules but of a very high quality. At the center was what looked like a five-story administrative building that somebody had decided to paint sage green. To the right and left, two-story wings stretched out. They had the look of warehouses or hangars with no windows but massive doors. And at about a mile's distance on my right, I could see an airfield.

The lead Land Rover pulled in in front of what I had

decided was the admin building. The driver climbed out and was indicating that I should park beside him, and his boys were taking up positions around me as I pulled in.

However rich Drake was, even if he had Elon Musk backing him, there was no way he could pull off an operation like this without the collusion of at least some departments of the United States, and specifically the infamous military industrial *intelligence* complex.

I swung down as the second Land Rover pulled in on my other side, and those boys also climbed out and covered me. It was overkill. They knew I was unarmed, and if I wanted to do anything, I'd have to take on and defeat eight trained, well-armed soldiers within the confines of a camp which was effectively a high security prison. But the point Drake and Santa Maria were making was that they were able to go for overkill, it was effortless for them, and they could afford that and a lot more.

A captain and four grunts accompanied me. The captain led the way, and I noted that he was about the same size and build as I was. The four grunts took up positions, one at each corner. We crossed a large foyer with a green marble floor. There were not many people. A guy at what looked like a reception desk, studying his computer and drinking coffee, ignored us as we crossed the floor toward a bank of elevators.

We rode the nearest one to the fifth floor, and I was marched through a large, open area where people who did not look like islanders were working at desks with computers. I was marched down a corridor that branched off that space, and at the end, the captain knocked on a large door made of dark wood. It buzzed, and he opened it.

"Sir, Mr. Bauer is here. He is not armed. He says he wants to speak with you and Governor Santa Maria."

There was a muttered response. The captain stepped aside, and I was delivered into the office. It was big by any standards. It must have been more than twenty feet from the door to where Drake was sitting behind a Nimitz class desk, and he gave an upward nod to the captain.

"You can take your men, Captain."

I heard the door close behind me and took a moment to look around. On my left there was an area that was essentially a library with a nest of leather armchairs set around a coffee table and at least two thousand books set in dark, mahogany shelves that went from floor to ceiling.

On my right there was what looked like an original Spanish credenza with a couple of silver trays bearing a variety of decanters and bottles. Above it was an original Picasso. I looked across the room at Drake and smiled. He had a big bandage and an even bigger bruise on his forehead.

"Mr. Bauer, I hope you are not here with violent intent this time. I am told you are here to make a deal. As a courtesy I have dismissed the soldiers, but be in no doubt, the slightest sign of violence on your behalf and you will be killed instantly."

I nodded and walked to the middle of the room, where I could see both him and Santa Maria.

"I tend only to kill people who try to kill me. I'm sensitive that way. Do I have to make this deal standing up, or are you going to offer me a chair?"

I walked over to the nest of chairs and looked down at Santa Maria in his tweed jacket and brocade vest. I sat. A moment later, I heard Drake sigh. He rose from his chair and crossed the room. He sat next to Santa Maria.

"Explain to me, Mr. Bauer, one good reason why I should not call my men and have them take you outside and shoot you right now."

"For the same reason you didn't have your men shoot me on the road when I arrived." I pointed around me. "You think I don't know that it would be impossible for you to set up and run this operation without the authorization of extremely senior, unelected figures back home? Do you think I am stupid enough to think the NSA, the CIA, and the British GCHQ don't know you're here, doing this?"

I sat back in my chair and crossed my legs.

"More to the point, Drake, do you think I am not aware of the shitfest that would hit the fan if Congress and the general public found out about this? If Europe, China, and Russia heard about this?" I pointed at him. "I am not dead because you need to know—" I paused and repeated it. "You *need* to know who sent me here, who I am working for, why they sent me, and above all, what happens if I contact them and, equally, what happens if I don't contact them. You haven't killed me because you need that information. And you will not torture me because you *need* to know the information is accurate and reliable."

I smiled and addressed Santa Maria for the first time.

"So if you are hoping to negotiate from a position of strength, think again."

It was Drake who answered. "And yet," he said and gestured at me with an open palm, "here you are, wanting to make a deal. And that means, Mr. Bauer, that you want something. What do you want, and what do you offer in return?"

"I'll tell you first what I'm offering. Then I'll tell you what I want in return. I am going to tell you who sent me, why they sent me, and how much they already know. I am going to tell you who organized the mission and what strings he or she pulls on the hill and in the Pentagon." I smiled. "This is not somebody you want to upset. I will tell you how much information

I have already been able to transmit and what happens if my transmissions go off line for more than a certain period of time. Most of all, I will tell you what *we* can do to ensure that your operation keeps chugging along and being productive."

Santa Maria spoke for the first time. "Who's 'we'?"

I pointed at him, at Drake, and at myself. "We."

"You are out of your mind."

I gave him the dead eye for ten seconds—it's a long time if you count them out.

"Am I? Let me tell you something, Santa Maria. I am going to stand up and walk to that door. The minute my heart stops pumping, the second my brain stops making electrical charges, this mine, your processing plants and your labs will be blown into the sea by four F-35s. There will be nothing left of you but the slime inside your heads."

"You're bluffing."

"Suits me. I was opposed to making the deal anyway."

I stood. Drake said, "Sit down, Mr. Bauer."

I regarded him a moment but stayed standing. "You want to give me a reason why I should?"

"We will proceed for now on the assumption that you are not bluffing. Frankly, it seems to me to be an almost impossible bluff to pull off. You are in here, you are unarmed, surrounded by highly trained, well-armed military personnel, and you have come here voluntarily. I don't honestly see what you can hope to achieve unless, as you say, you have some kind of external resource. I, personally, am keen to know what that is."

"I bet you are at that." I turned to Santa Maria. "What about you? You think your pal Drake is a fool for playing along? You think I'm going to lull you into a false sense of security and then turn all ninja on you and kill a hundred men with my bare hands and feet?"

His face had flushed pink. "All right, Mr. Bauer! Sit down. Tell us. Who are your employers?"

"Oh, sure." I sat down. "Shall I tell you what color my panties are, too?" I turned back to Drake. "I'm going to talk to you. You seem to be in the real world. This clown is off with the fairies. I'm guessing you've done your share of negotiating in your time. So you know nobody gives something for nothing. So if I have five key pieces of information that you need, I am not going to give you that without some guarantee that you are not going to kill me."

"Clearly. So what do you want?"

"For a start, in exchange for who I work for, I want safe passage out of I-Takka for Marguerite, the owner of the St. Homer Hotel, and Camilla, her daughter. And I want the guys who beat Marguerite."

Santa Maria expostulated, "What do you mean, you *want* them?"

"I want them right there, in the middle of that floor. I don't care if they are armed or unarmed, and I don't give a solitary goddamn if they defend themselves. I am going to kill them. Are we clear?"

"It's infantile."

"Yeah, Santa Maria, that's the kind of guy I am. I see a man hit a woman, and it gets to me. It's my Galahad complex. You have any more observations to make?"

His cheeks went pink, but he shut up. Drake said, "How do you propose we do this?"

I held up my index finger. "First, you bring those sons of bitches to me, the guy who beat her and whoever was with him to hold his beer. While I am explaining the finer points of chivalry to them, you send a car to get Marguerite and Camilla, and you have your men prepare one of your planes for take-off.

As soon as they get here, you bring them to me, and then you put both of them on a flight to Fort Lauderdale. When I am sure they have taken off safely, I tell you who I work for and what the purpose of my mission is. When I hear that they have landed and your pilot is on his way back, then we move on to stage two. For that, you're going to have to reconnect the phones."

The two men stared at each other for a long moment. Eventually Santa Maria shrugged. "It costs us nothing."

"Fine." Drake rose and went to his desk, where he picked up a telephone receiver.

"Prepare AC4. I want Ibanez and Carter. We need an immediate flight plan departing imminently, destination Fort Lauderdale with two passengers. Contact the FFA and get priority clearance. Tell Ibanez I want to know as soon as he takes off from Fort Lauderdale on his return flight. Oh, and Grant, reactivate the telephone lines. We have the situation under control."

He hung up and pressed a button on his desk. A soldier came in and saluted.

"Go and collect Marguerite Owens and her daughter from the hotel St. Homer." He glanced at me. "Are they expecting to be collected?"

I smiled and made it a little smug, just to annoy. "Yeah, I told hem you'd be showing up."

He suppressed a sigh and added, "And send Petersen up with Rogers and Günter."

TWELVE

Petersen and Rogers and Günter knocked on the door about twelve minutes later. They shuffled in looking worried, and Petersen, the first in, frowned when he saw me sitting there like one of the guys, watching him. He shifted his gaze to Drake and said, "Sir?"

Drake looked away. He and Santa Maria exchanged a glance. Drake sighed, and I stood up and walked over so I was standing just a foot from Petersen, looking him in the eye. I was playing for time, but I also wanted Drake and Santa Maria to see what was coming next, for its psychological effect.

A guy who is a prisoner in a high security military prison, surrounded by razor wire and over a hundred armed soldiers with no backup or external support does not behave the way I was about to behave. It takes belief, belief in backup, in reinforcements, in the strength of some kind of support system behind you.

Either that or to be completely out of your mind and not give a damn.

I held Petersen's eye. He could see what I was doing, and he could see that Drake and Santa Maria were not stopping me. So did that mean that to defy me was to defy them? He didn't know. So he waited, hoping for a signal from his boss.

"You like beating up women, Petersen?"

He didn't answer me. He looked past me at Drake, who was studying the wall.

"Mr. Drake, sir? I was following orders, sir..."

"I'm asking you a question, Petersen," I snarled. "Do you enjoy beating up women? Because I have a theory. I think that men who beat up women are basically sissies. I think you have to be some kind of a cowardly, woman-hating pansy to beat up on a woman." He swallowed hard. I pressed him. "What's the matter, Petersen? You haven't got the balls to defend yourself without your boss's permission? You're only tough with women?"

I raised my voice and took the opportunity to humiliate Drake in front of his men and his partner. "Hey! Drake! Tell this pussy he's allowed to defend himself."

His voice, when it came, would have made polar bears shiver.

"You may defend yourself, Petersen."

The schmuck was caught for a second in a state of confusion. It's a pretty good rule of thumb to create a moment of confusion for your enemy before you strike.

When tough guys confront each other chest to chest, nose to nose, they're actually too close to hit each other with any effect—or so they think. So they resort to pushing before they start throwing punches. But if you just turn your left heel out a couple of inches and drive a left hook in and up, deep into the other guy's liver, the fight ends right there.

He didn't see it coming. How could he? I was too close, and there was nothing to telegraph it. It ruptured his liver, he went crimson, and all the veins in his neck and his head bulged. He went down, dying slowly and painfully on the floor.

I stood, looking at the other two. “How about you guys? You like beating up on women?” I pointed at the biggest of the two. He had blue eyes and freckles. I said, “You Günter?”

There was defiance in his expression. “Sir, Mr. Drake, sir. Do we have to take this? Can we defend ourselves? We was just—”

“You heard the man! You can defend yourselves! Show me what you got, Snow Drop.”

He lunged at me. It was his obvious move. He was bigger and heavier than me, and he figured if he took me down, he could start breaking things like my arms and my back. That’s why you always keep your heavy artillery at the front. A guy who’s charging to take you down has his arms open to grab you. He’s wide open. You lunge forward with a straight right to the jaw, and however big he is, he’s going down.

But I didn’t want Günter down just yet. I had time to kill and a lesson to impart. So instead of the jaw, I struck his throat with the thenar web. That’s the inner edge of the hand between the index finger and the thumb, and when it smashes into the windpipe, the guy thinks he is going to die of asphyxia. For Günter, that impact came with the combined weight of his charge and my lunge.

Günter was going to die, but not right then, and not of asphyxia. As he staggered away clutching at his throat, I stepped past him. Rogers had taken a defensive position because he had no idea what the hell was going to happen next. What happened next was a roundhouse kick with the instep delivered to the side of his left knee. It was fast and savagely hard, and I felt the cartilage crunch as it connected.

It was a second at most that he gasped and hopped on his

right leg. By that time, I was behind him. I put my right arm around his neck and gripped my left bicep. My left forearm went behind his neck, and I squeezed. He struggled for no more than twenty seconds. Then he went limp. I laid him face down on the floor, and for good measure I stamped on the back of his neck.

Günter was getting his breath back and struggling to his feet. I delivered a right hook right through his cheekbone, where it hurts but won't do much to a tough guy like Günter. I jabbed him a couple of times on the nose, driving him back to a corner where he was not clearly visible to Drake and Santa Maria, and when he swung a big right but telegraphed it a week ahead of delivery, I weaved, trapped it across his chest, and smacked him on the nose again twice, driving him farther back into the corner. Now he looked nervous.

I narrowed my eyes. "You scared, Günter? You think Marguerite was scared with three big, tough pansies beating her up?" I smiled. "Time to die, asshole."

I feinted with my right to his face. He tried to block it with both hands, and I drove another savage left hook into his liver. He fell against the wall, gasping. I crowded in on him and drove a barrage of right and left hooks into his already ruptured vital organ. And while I was at it, I slipped his Glock from its holster and into my waistband, under my jacket.

He slumped to the floor, and I put him out of his misery with a sharp heel to the back of his neck.

I returned to the table. Santa Maria was watching me with a curious mix of disgust and excitement. With Drake it was just plain disgust.

"It was the way I was raised," I told him. "You don't hit women. They are the mothers of the race, you know? We're supposed to respect them."

His face flushed. "You are so full of shit, Bauer! I should have you executed right now!"

"Yeah, you probably should, Drake. But at what cost? That's what you need to ask yourself. At what cost?"

He stared at me for a long time, trying to weigh up odds he had no figures for. In the end, he snarled, "Who do you work for?"

I sat and smiled at no one in particular. "You're not going to believe me," I said.

Santa Maria gave one of those 'I told you so' laughs. Drake growled, "Try me."

"I work for the Department for the Elimination of Abominations, Terrorists, and the Heinous."

Santa Maria said, "DEATH."

Drake went very still and narrowed his eyes. "Be very careful, Bauer. You are going too far. I am tolerating this because you have promised something in return. Keep playing this stupid game and you die."

"I told you you wouldn't believe me. The department exists. It was created in the late '90s as a joint project between the United Kingdom and the United States as a response to what had happened in Croatia and Serbia after the collapse of Yugoslavia and what had happened in Iraq. There was an understanding that there were people who were beyond the reach of the law but who should rightly be eliminated. Former British Director of Special Forces Brigadier Jonathan Northward-Watson was promoted to major general and appointed director. He was a man with a sense of humor, and he came up with the name. 'An acronym for every eventuality.' That's what he said.

"The department was later absorbed into the Five Eyes. You probably know, as a defense contractor, that the Five Eyes presents itself as a loose, cooperative group but is in fact one of the three foundation stones of Western defense and an integral part of the military industrial intelligence complex that governs the Western World. DEATH is a branch of that organization."

Santa Maria said, "Is it credible?"

Drake muttered, "I've heard rumors. But the name..." He trailed off. "In intelligence they play with names to set false trails. Omega, ODNI, ODIN, Cobra... Yes, it is barely credible. What is your purpose here? Why were you sent?"

I raised my eyebrows high. "Really? Seriously? You have three hundred enslaved workers here, you have deliberately located your operation outside of any official jurisdiction, and you are murdering children just for fun..."—I paused and watched Drake glance at Santa Maria—"...and you wonder why the Department for the Elimination of Abominations, Terrorists, and the Heinous is investigating you? Well, maybe it's because you constitute a heinous abomination."

He seemed not to hear. He said "Five Eyes?" like it was a question.

"Yes, Drake, Five Eyes, the most sophisticated, technologically advanced listening system known to man. You may contribute to it, Drake, and as you are mining and processing lithium in these quantities, I figure you do, but believe me, you have no idea just how smart Five Eyes is, how advanced, or how far they have taken AI."

It was a bluff, but I figured it had a better than fifty percent chance of hitting home, and it did. He looked worried. One thing was a loudmouth special ops guy pulling a ballsy bluff. Quite another was a classified department drawing on intelligence from the Five Eyes.

The timing of the arrival of Marguerite and Camilla could not have been better. Drake and Santa Maria were still agonizing over what was happening, still needing to pump me for information, but they were forced to act on the next stage of my demands if they wanted that information.

There was a tap at the door. The captain who'd escorted me earlier came in, stared at the bodies scattered on the floor, then at Drake and me. I snapped, "Get this trash out of here, Captain."

The captain looked at Drake for confirmation. He got it. "Get them out of here. Have you got Marguerite and Camilla?"

"Yes, sir. They're here."

I said, "Bring them in and get those damned bodies incinerated."

He glanced at Drake, got a nod, and turned to snap orders at men waiting outside the door. "Bring them in and get these bodies out of here! Take them to the incinerator!"

I smiled. It was only a small step, but next time I gave that officer an order, he'd obey it without seeking confirmation.

Marguerite and Camilla came in. They watched the bodies being dragged out with that particular kind of horror that is turning to a very dark kind of tedium, where half the horror is because you are growing accustomed to it. They both stopped and stared at me. With Marguerite, it was an expression of disbelief. With Camilla it was an expression of betrayal. I ignored both and spoke to the wall, like I didn't give a damn.

"You're about to board a plane to Fort Lauderdale. You will be met there by an American officer who will identify himself as representing Harry Bauer. Do exactly as he says, and he will keep you safe."

Camilla said, "I don't believe you. You're with them."

I turned to her and raised an eyebrow. "You want to explain to me why I am putting you on a plane?"

"To kill us." She pointed at Santa Maria and Drake. "You're with them."

"Listen to me, Camilla. I'm not with them; we're just working something out. You saw those three guys they just dragged out? You recognized them as the men who beat your mom. So if I could do that to them here in this office, you want to explain to me why I would waste the fuel and money on a transport plane when I could deal with the two of you right here and now? Be smart, Camilla. Go with your mom. Whatever they ask you, whatever they tell you, you play dumb and tell them Harry Bauer sent you off the island, you don't know why, and they should talk to me. You understand that?"

She didn't answer, but she took her mom's arm and held it tightly. Marguerite said, "We understand."

I looked at the captain. "Get these women on that plane. Then I want you right back here, and you stand guard outside that door. We have things to discuss, and nobody, I mean *nobody*, disturbs us. Any questions?"

He hesitated, looking for Drake, but Drake was out of sight. He said, "No, sir."

"Then get to it, Captain!" I turned to Marguerite and Camilla. "Scram!"

They filed out, and the door closed. Santa Maria and Drake were staring at me. They felt safe because they were still in charge and we were deep within the massive, heavily guarded complex that was the Company. They were surrounded by guns and soldiers and barbed wire and steel walls. Even so, they had the acronym WTF glowing on their foreheads.

"I am assuming that you are having this conversation recorded, but the room is soundproofed and you haven't got some grunt listening to every word we say."

Santa Maria said, "That is correct."

Drake said, "What the fuck are you playing at, Bauer?"

He went to stand, but I pointed at him and said, "Wait." He stopped. I went on, "You feel safe and secure because you are effectively surrounded by a high-tech fortress. But I ask you, aren't you overlooking something?"

He frowned. "Overlooking what?"

I pulled the Glock from behind my back. "I'm on the inside."

I plugged him through the heart. I could have shot him in the head, but I needed his face. As he sank awkwardly to the floor, I turned the gun on Santa Maria. All the blood had drained from his face, and he had turned a waxy cream color and was suddenly sweating profusely. Keeping the gun trained on him, I moved over to Drake. I fished in his pocket and pulled out his cell. I showed it his face and reset it to recognize my face instead. Then I smiled at Santa Maria.

"So," I said. "Let's move on to the next stage."

THIRTEEN

"YOU WERE IN SPECIAL FORCES."

I smiled. "Shucks, is it that obvious? Take your shoes off."

"You know the value of violence."

"I know the value of violence, Santa Maria, and so will you if you don't take your damned shoes off."

He busied himself with his laces and slipped off his shoes.

"You fought the Taliban in Afghanistan."

"Thanks. How tall am I? Take off your pants and your jacket."

"What are you going to do?"

"Explain the value of violence."

"That's not necessary. I am completely compliant."

"I know. So do as you're told."

He started to strip as I pulled the laces from Drake's shoes.

"Violence is a language." He said it as he pulled down his pants. "It is the most effective universal language. They say mathematics"—now he was pulling off his jacket—"but that is like saying Proto-Indo-European is a universal language. A language that only the initiates speak is not universal. What now?"

He stood, huge, in his socks, his shirt, and his boxer shorts.

"Put your hands behind your back."

He turned his back on me and crossed his hands behind him. "The West suffers from blind stupidity," he said.

I tied his left wrist with Drake's shoelace and bound it tightly to his right, muttering, "No argument from me on that score."

"We believe that everybody thinks like us. You can see this in Palestine and Israel, in the Middle East, Afghanistan, and Pakistan..."

He trailed off. Maybe because he sensed that I had stopped. I had intended to lay him facedown and tie his ankles, then run his belt from the binding on his ankles to his wrists and pull it tight. But something in what he was saying was getting to me. I sat him down and bound his ankles with the other shoelace, then stood and said, "OK, Santa Maria, what are you trying to tell me?"

He leaned forward, and suddenly his face was alive and intense. "After the Second World War, Mr. Bauer, the West was crippled by a wave of profound, enervating, *paralyzing* naïve stupidity! We had become civilized. *We* had embraced the values of equality, of democracy, of compassionate pragmatism. Do you know what I mean when I say that Christ's revolution had risen through the ferment of lies of the Christian churches that had hijacked it?"

"No. It sounds like you're spouting bullshit."

He closed his eyes and sighed. "This is important, Mr. Bauer. Pay attention." I almost smiled. Here was a guy who was disarmed, bound hand and foot, half naked and on the threshold of execution, and he was lecturing me on the history of Western ethics and telling me to pay attention. For just a moment he reminded me of me.

"Speak a language I can understand."

"The religions of Abraham teach subjugation, obedience, and the virtues of self sacrifice and suffering. They are predicated on a god who is cruel and vengeful, vain, irrational, and even infantile in His tantrums. But Jesus attempted to teach a different ideology. He tried to teach about a God who was kind and forgiving and compassionate. He taught that men should be kind and forgiving and compassionate."

"I'm running out of patience, Santa Maria. Get to the point."

"Bear with me. This is important."

"You said that. Get to the important part."

"It was only when Christ's teachings were taken out of the Middle East, taken, indeed, out of the Mediterranean, and transposed to northwestern Europe that his message was truly understood."

"I'm done."

I moved to roll him on his belly, but he kept talking. "The Jews found a way to escape from Elohim through sophistry and intellectualism. They interpreted and analyzed and found ways to understand Jehovah as a god of love, though they never accepted Jesus as the Messiah."

He managed to stop me again, and I paused and listened.

"The Christians did the same, but not through sophistry and intellectualism. After more than a thousand years of cruelty and monstrous abuse, in that northwestern corner of Europe, they found a different path to the same place the Jews were at. They found a god of love and peace and forgiveness through Christian fundamentalism."

"If you are trying to tell me something, Santa Maria, tell it."

"But Islam entrenched itself and exalted that god of vengeance and cruelty." He laughed, and it was startling. "Of course, they tell us, 'Allah is a god of love and forgiveness!' Yes, of course, *if you embrace the Islamic faith!* But if you do not, the Koran tells us again and again that nothing is so loathsome in the eyes of Allah as an infidel, and those who fail to convert will spend eternity being cruelly tortured while the angels watch and laugh."

He edged forward with an almost crazed passion in his eyes.

"We moved through the Renaissance, the Enlightenment, and the Industrial Revolution. We developed the Rule of Law, political accountability, universal suffrage, freedom of speech..." He shook his head in quick, lateral jerks. "Nobody had ever done that before. *Nobody!*"

Either he was getting at something or he was crazy. I was beginning to lean toward the second option. He pressed on.

"In the twelve thousand years since the flood, Mr. Bauer, nobody had ever done what we did..." He leaned farther, staring into my face like he was trying to drive a thought into my mind by pure telepathic willpower. "*But we didn't understand that!* Darwin got into our heads! Evolution! Evolution! What we had done was just part of evolution! And if we had evolved this way, then surely everybody must! But they didn't... And they haven't..."

"Is there a point to all this, Santa Maria?"

"Yes."

"Glad to hear it. Get on your belly on the sofa, face down."

"Listen to me!"

"For Christ's sake, Santa Maria! What the hell is it?"

"Do you understand what I am telling you? We are negotiating with people we do not understand! We think they have our same pragmatic values. We think they are motivated by wealth, by privilege, by comfort and security, *but they are not!* They are motivated by evil, by hatred! They have black souls! We think, 'We have brought them to the negotiating table. That is so good. Now we will have pragmatic negotiations because they want to end this terrible conflict...'" He sat, shaking his head. "But no, Mr. Bauer. *They want war! They thrive on conflict! They want blood! They want revenge!*"

"Why are you telling me all this? What are you driving at?"

"Pakistan has nuclear capability. Russia is going to give Iran nuclear capability. They have ballistic missiles capable of covering huge distances at tremendous speeds..." His face flushed, his eyes staring with an insane light. "And while we focus on their missiles, their Hashishim swarm into Europe and Britain disguised as refugees and protected by the Human Rights Charters, they infiltrate our national and local legislatures, they become voters and then voting communities, and sway our politicians and soon, soon..."

He trailed off.

"Soon what?"

"What happened to Troy when the Achaeans entered the city in the great wooden horse? What I am telling you, Mr. Bauer, is that the Trojan horse that has been deployed against us is our own civilization. That we have lost our ruthlessness and we need to recover it. You rail against us for what we have created here, but do you not see that we *need* to become ruthless? That Iran and Russia, and the whole culture of Islam, must be destroyed or they will destroy us!"

I arched an eyebrow at him. "You are telling me that you have created this whole setup, the mine, the processing plant, the slaves, the child labor, as part of an honorable, noble enterprise to protect the West from the encroaching evil of Islam and Sharia Law?"

He stared at me for a long time with slightly bulging eyes.

"There are those of us," he said at last. Then, "Billionaires. It's like a club."

"A *club?*"

He gave a small laugh, like a simper. "People like you, you might buy a jacket on the spur of the moment, or go on holiday to Egypt as a caprice. We send an electric car into space or set up a colony on Mars. It's a different perception of reality."

"You're out of your mind."

"No." He shook his head. "I'm out of *your* mind. You can't begin to imagine what it's like to be me."

A sudden rage welled up inside me, and I pointed toward the window at the vast complex outside. "This is a *caprice?* You have stolen people's lives! You have enslaved them, destroyed them, murdered children! And this is a *caprice?*"

"It's beyond your understanding—"

"What is? That you feel entitled to rob people's lives and kill them because you have fifty billion dollars in the bank? Yeah! That is beyond my understanding, you son of a bitch!"

"The project is not a caprice, Mr. Bauer. And there is no need for personal insults. I have perhaps expressed myself badly. But where you, or people like you, may sit in a bar and watch the news and feel powerless to do anything about the events in the world, Bill, Elon—we tend to avoid the company of Mark—and Jeff, for that matter—but I digress. As I was saying, Bill, Elon, I, and a few others you may not have heard of, when we see a situation on the world stage, we know we can do something about it. Bill is very concerned about overpopulation. So is Elon, and they are looking at possible ways of solving that problem. Personally I think they are on the wrong track. I think we need a cull."

"A cull..."

He shrugged. "Honestly, yes. There are too many of us. Far, far too many of us. So we need to identify the regressive elements, those who will hold back our growth and development, those who have failed to develop civilized, advanced societies, those who are crippled by stupidity and superstition—" He laughed suddenly, and again it was startling. "I mean we are talking about nine-tenths of the human race, but with the appropriate technology, we could solve climate change and overpopulation in a couple of years with no negative impact on the global economy."

"What the hell are you doing in this place? Are you developing weapons of mass destruction?"

He laughed again. "No! No, nothing like that. It's only in the early stages of development. We are just developing the electronics and of course the batteries for the satellite mounted... umm..." He must have seen the expression on my face because he trailed off and turned waxy again. "It's theoretical. All very much theoretical."

"You are developing next generation lithium batteries and stockpiling them."

He swallowed hard. "Yes."

"The experiments," I said. "The experiments on people."

He was shaking his head, and suddenly he looked close to tears. "You have to understand. We face an existential threat. Islam is a cancer. Worse. It is a virus that attacks the brain—"

"The experiments."

"It's the future! Whether we like it or not, and we have to get there first! Russia and Chine have no constraints. They can go to the Steppes, to the deserts, to Mongolia, and there is no one to stop their research! Can you imagine Iran with intelligent, self-guiding nuclear missiles?"

"That's science fiction! Tell me—"

He cut across me, screaming, his face flushed red, "*We left science fiction behind! Are you blind? Can't you see? The craziest science fiction does not come close to what we are experimenting with!*"

The room went silent. I said quietly, "What are you experimenting with?"

"You're going to kill me."

"You can count on it if you don't start talking."

"Through some misguided sense of moral outrage—"

"Three, two—"

"The marriage of artificial intelligence with biological components."

I sat slowly. "What?"

"Someone is going to do it sooner or later. We *have* to be ahead of the game. Emotions are organic, Mr. Bauer. If I remove your adrenal glands and control your dopamine, serotonin, and blood pressure, you will think with utter clarity, but you will have virtually no emotions. If in addition I can install AI receptors in your brain and unicellular computers with programs written in protein by photon lasers to perform particular tasks like complex mathematical calculations, your brain will be like the brain of a god but with no motivational will of its own. We could program your motivation into you and install you as the pilot of a drone—or an F-35!"

"Or a nuclear missile."

"Yes. The potential is beyond imagining."

"Who is running this? Who knows about it?"

He jerked his head at Drake's body crumpled like an old suit on the floor. "Obviously it was all compartmentalized. You killed the only man who had those links, about the only man who had all the information you want."

I studied him a moment. "I am not going to kill you," I said.

His face twisted with a volatile cocktail of hope, terror, and mistrust. I shook my head and went on.

"I am going to have you testify before Congress. You will have every hot man available to the military industrial intelligence complex out to get you. Your life won't be worth a damn, but your death will be worth millions. I am not going to do them that favor. You are going to tell Congress and the American people exactly what this project was."

"Was?" His face was like a lemon twist of tears and laughter. "You really think they won't replace Drake and me within the week? You really believe you can beat them?"

"I don't know if I can beat them, Santa Maria, but I know for damn sure that I would rather die fighting them than live being one of them."

"Naïve. You're so naïve."

"Lie on your belly on the sofa."

I trussed him up so he could not move, stuffed two pairs of socks in his mouth, made sure he could breathe, and made a thorough search of Drake's desk. I didn't find anything of much interest, though I did find what I was hoping for hanging on the wall in a slim, black frame. It was a plan of the facility, and two large warehouses were highlighted as storage facilities for both batteries and raw lithium.

I paused to look at him, watching me from where he lay. I thought about killing him there and then, but he was right. They would replace him and Drake within a week. Whatever I did, however risky, it had to be more permanent. I headed for the door, thinking about the word permanent. I am not a religious man. I have seen too much senseless suffering, too many innocent children pay the price for human stupidity and cruelty. But as I reached for the handle, the thought came to me that we were indeed paying the price for consuming the fruit of the tree of knowledge. Technological advancement, even to a point that went beyond science fiction, as Santa Maria had said, into the realms of fantasy, did not lead to higher levels of morality and goodness. It led instead to men questioning the very existence of morality and goodness.

Man's objective was, always had been, and always would be, power; and the means of acquiring it would always be violence.

That was the Law.

FOURTEEN

I STEPPED OUT AND LET THE HEAVY, SOUNDPROOF door close behind me. The captain watched me like a man who has better things to do than stand outside a door.

"Captain, I want two men posted on this door. What is going down in there today is classified above top secret. We'll be in conference with the president of the United States, John Ratcliff at the CIA, and Air Force General Dan Caine, chairman of the Joint Chiefs of Staff. Nobody, but *nobody* goes in there. You understand?"

"Yes, sir."

He was still a little confused, but he'd seen me giving orders and Drake and Santa Maria taking it. I clearly had authority, and so he wasn't about to question it. He made a call on his radio, and five minutes later, two gorillas with stone faces untroubled by thought stood outside the door and formed a barrier the Heavenly Hosts couldn't get through.

I told the captain, "Now take me to hangars eighteen and twenty-three."

He baulked. My face told him he might die, and he snapped, "Yes, sir. Right away."

He led me down in the elevator and through the foyer. It was busier now. There were maybe a dozen people. Some were walking through like they had something to do somewhere else. There were a woman and two guys standing beside the reception desk discussing papers on a clipboard the woman was holding. There was a guy cleaning the windows and another polishing the marble floor with a buggy he was driving. It might have been any office block downtown.

We stepped out into the sunshine. I made a point of ignoring the activity up at the airfield. I said, "Is it far?"

The captain looked surprised. "Ten minute walk, more or less."

"We'll take my Jeep."

His gut told him it wasn't wise, but his brain couldn't find a reason. And before he could give it much thought, I was behind the wheel, firing up the engine. He climbed in the passenger seat. and I took off as he slammed the door.

"Captain, I am assuming two things: You possess very limited information about this operation"—I glanced at him—"because of the very nature of the operation itself. But I am also assuming, given your rank, that you have made the logical deductions and are aware that this is a clandestine operation draped in plausible deniability."

"The next one on the right, sir."

I slowed, took the turn, and saw a very large hangar ahead with the number 18 emblazoned over a vast, rolling steel door. I pulled up outside and killed the engine, then sat staring at the vast prefab in front of me.

"What's your name, Captain?"

"Nicholas Wise, sir."

"Captain Wise, we are about to see some major, global changes. If you've been watching, you will have seen that our warrior nation is girding its loins for what it's best at—war. Some players who thought they were powerful, who thought they had the West on the ropes, who thought they could bring terror to the world, are about to get their asses whipped. Drake is not a man who gives out a lot of praise, but he spoke well of you. If what he said about you is true, there could be important opportunities for you in what is coming up. So I have a question for you. Are you ready to seize those opportunities?"

He didn't think twice. He didn't bat an eyelash. "Yes, sir. Absolutely." He was mine.

"Good. I need to know I have chosen the right man." I opened the door. "Let's go. Show me this place."

We climbed out, and he approached the massive door ahead of me. There was a smaller, hinged door inserted within the larger one. He showed his palm to a screen, punched in a code, and stated, "Captain Nicholas Wise."

The smaller door buzzed and clicked open. He pushed in. I followed, and he flipped a switch. High up in the ceiling, strip lights flickered and flooded the vast, cavernous area with a stark, white glow.

Far over on the left, there was a series of what looked like offices and/or store rooms, but the walls ahead and on the right were stacked to a height of maybe a hundred and fifty or two hundred feet with twenty-gallon plastic drums. The drums were maybe twenty-five or thirty deep. They were held on large, wooden pallets, and there were too many to count.

"This is raw lithium?"

"Yes."

"How much?"

"We have one thousand five hundred tons here. In hangar

twenty-three, we have five thousand batteries of varying times. Some of them are prototypes, like the Omega Batteries, which will drive turbines, and then there are the carbon-lithium batteries which use carbon nanotubes—"

"OK, Captain..." I trailed off. Outside, I could hear a jet accelerating down the runway, then fading into the sky. Marguerite, Camilla, and the doc were on their way. I pulled my cell from my pocket, saw I had signal, and sent a secure, coded message to the brigadier:

Marguerite and Camilla, witnesses, on way to safety at Fort Lauderdale. Please meet and make safe.

I sent it and told the captain, "Show me the batteries."

"Yes, sir."

We stepped out into the broad space between the rows of hangars. I told him, "Leave it open. I'll be coming in and out for a while."

"It's against procedure, sir."

"Don't sweat it, Captain. I'll take full responsibility. We haven't got time to register my bios right now."

He looked unhappy but said, "Yes sir" and led me across to hangar twenty-three, dodging a Jeep on the way. He went through the same procedure, and the smaller door opened. Inside, it was a similar setup, only smaller. There were hundreds of wooden pallets stacked along the walls, all loaded up with a wide variety of batteries. Some looked like small missiles, and others were packed in cartons, twenty to a box. Still other were held in hardened plastic housings.

"I'm trying to think how we do this," I said. "Come."

I led him across the floor at a quick march and opened the door of what looked like an office with a long window. There was nobody in there. I said, "Come in and close the door."

He stepped in, and as he did so, I smashed my knuckles

into his windpipe. His face went purple, and his eyes bulged. I followed up with an elbow to the tip of his jaw. He went straight down, and I stamped on the back of his neck to make sure he was dead. I took his uniform and put it on, then opened the door and stepped out. I crossed the massive space, listening to my new boots echo all the way up the walls and into the ceiling, and stepped out of the hangar.

I walked without hurrying back across to where my Jeep was parked outside 18. I resisted the temptation to look around, reached under the chassis like it was a perfectly normal thing to do, loosened the rucksack I had strapped there, and carried it into hangar 18.

Bringing it had been a risk, but it had been a calculated risk that had paid off. I had been confident that once I told them I wanted to make a deal, they would want to talk to me. They had too many important, unanswered questions about who I was and why I was there. And what played in my favor was that when I had attacked Drake at his home in the Cala, my weaponry had been limited, to say the least. They had me in custody, they had my Sig and my knife, and I was talking to them. They had no need to scan beneath the chassis of my car. If they had, the worst thing that could have happened was that I would lose what little ordnance I had.

As it was, it had paid off.

I made my way across the big, echoing hangar to the center of the massive stack of drums. I took out two pounds of C4, mashed them into a cake, took a chunk the size of a damson plum, and dropped it in my pocket. I stuffed the rest out of sight under the wooden pallet, pressed onto the floor so that the main force of the blast would drive up, at about two thousand six hundred degrees Fahrenheit into the raw lithium.

I stabbed in the detonator and connected it to my phone.

The next step was trickier. Special ops military bases are close-knit places. It's like your home. Everyone knows everybody else, and everyone is aware. You won't get a stranger walking through an SAS base unchallenged.

Big, regular Army or Air Force bases are different. They deal in hundreds, sometimes thousands of men and women, from general to grunts, mechanics to cleaners and civilian admin. This place hung somewhere between the two, with the added advantage to me that everything was compartmentalized. If you saw or heard something you did not understand, you kept your nose *out*. You did not stick it in. So I slung my rucksack over my shoulder, climbed into the Jeep, and rolled sedately down the broad, open track that led past the hangars toward the barracks.

But before the barracks was that other place I had spotted, that was more like a small concentration camp.

I pulled up with the distorted shadow of my truck leaning through the heavy wooden posts and the barbed wire onto the dirt inside. I sat watching a while and noticed what had struck me earlier: There was nobody in there. I looked up at the guard towers. The mounted machine guns were there, but there was nobody manning them.

I spun the wheel and headed toward the main gate. Before I got there, I came to a broad, dirt track and turned right, following it along for maybe half a mile. On the way, I passed a truck headed in the opposite direction, back toward the complex, loaded with dirt. Then, up ahead, I saw two more trucks parked at the top of what at first glance looked like a vast crater. It was maybe a mile across with sheer faces on the inside.

As I got closer, I saw that the trucks were at the top of a broad track that descended into the mine, skirting the face in a descending spiral that grew ever narrower as it approached the bottom. The bottom I figured was over a thousand feet down.

Ascending that broad, spiral track was another truck, loaded with dirt. The two at the top were waiting for it to emerge so they could go down. Just beyond the nearest of the trucks was a prefab office. Outside it were a couple of men smoking cigarettes and talking. They had rifles leaning against the wall by their sides. Over on my left, there were a couple more, their rifles hung on their shoulders. One was looking down into the mine. The other was watching me.

I swung down from the Jeep. I reached in the back and retrieved the Tavor bullpup from my rucksack, flipped off the safety, slung it over my shoulder, and walked to the edge of the vast crater. Now I could see the workers. They were way down and looked like ants. I figured there must have been three hundred of them, the whole crew, scattered in small groups. That was why the concentration camp was empty. They were all here.

It was impossible for them to get out except by following the track, which would not only turn their one-mile climb into what must have been close to a twenty-mile uphill hike, it also made them easy targets for a small handful of gunmen.

"Can I help you, sir?"

The accent was South African. The tone was insolent. He was standing seven feet from me. He must have been six foot six, gym muscled and probably Zulu.

"Who's in charge here?"

His big, slightly yellow eyes said maybe he was going to throw me into the mine. Instead he looked past me and shouted, "Yo! Brookman! C'mere! Captain wants to talk to you!"

I watched him for a beat, and he watched me back. I spoke quietly.

"I want to talk to you, too. What's your name?" Before he could answer, I cut him short and added, "Tell your friend to get his ass over here too."

He turned to call his friend, and I said, "I asked you a question." He turned, and there was something like rage in his eyes. I said, "What is your name?"

"My name, sir, is Mr. Jim Brown."

"Call your friend over here, Brown."

I turned to Brookman, pointed over at the prefab, and raised my voice. "Bring that man over here, and anyone in the office."

He stopped, eyed my uniform from the distance, then turned back and shouted for the guy to join them. They both brought their rifles with them. Brown's friend had joined us.

As Brookman and his pal were arriving, Brown said, "You know, we are not part of the military. You have no—"

I cut him short. "Is that something you know?" He closed his mouth and narrowed his eyes. I went on. "Then you don't know shit, Brown." I pointed down the track toward the gate. "The moment you walk through that gate, you are whatever Mr. Drake and Mr. Santa Maria tell you you are. If they say you are shit, then you are shit. Do you understand that, or do I have to explain it to you in more detail?"

He didn't like it, but he recognized authority when he heard it, and he closed his mouth. I didn't. They had all gathered around and were frowning at me. I fixed my eyes on Brookman and spoke quietly.

"When you look at me, gentlemen"—I allowed the irony to ooze over the word—"you are looking at Mr. Drake and Mr. Santa Maria. I am here to review security."

"We haven't been notified—"

"Do I look like I give a damn, Brookman?" I didn't wait for an answer. "How many men have you got supervising this mine? What happens if there is trouble down there?"

"Just us four, but we—"

I never found out what they did or didn't do or were. The bullpup put three rounds through his chest in a quarter of a second. That's as long as it takes you to say "an."

By the time he realized he'd been shot, I'd put three more rounds into Mr. James Brown's barrel chest. Three more had gone through his pal by the time Brookman's friend had started reaching for his rifle. He took three more.

I could see the drivers of the two trucks staring at me. I let the X95 drop but left it hanging from my shoulder and marched toward the trucks. I was telling them I was not intending to shoot them, but I was holding their attention. I pointed at them in turn, one after the other.

"*This does not concern you! Continue with your work!*"

They both simultaneously looked to the front. I marched to the rear truck and shouted to him to lower his window. As he did so, I shot him in the head. It was an easy shot from less than three feet. I ran the fifteen feet that separated me from the cab of the other truck. He'd seen what I'd done and was spinning his wheel and starting to accelerate. All that did was bring him into range. Four rounds shattered the window and took off his head.

I didn't stop. I kept running till I came to the top of the track. The truck that was climbing the ramp was just forty yards from the top. All the driver could see was some jerk in a captain's uniform gesturing him to keep going. Maybe I made it look urgent because he accelerated. The early sun was reflecting on his windshield, so I let him get to twenty feet away before I emptied the last ten rounds into his head and chest.

I turned and ran back toward the Jeep. I wrenched open the rear passenger door and took out my remaining cakes of C4, stabbed a detonator in them, and ran to the prefab. There was no one in there, as I had expected. I dumped the C4 on the office computer and legged it back to the Jeep, stowed the bullpup, clambered behind the wheel, and drove back toward the admin building.

FIFTEEN

THE TWO SOLDIERS ON THE DOOR TRIED NOT TO frown at my uniform as I emerged from the elevator. They saluted me and stepped aside to let me in. I ignored them.

Inside, Santa Maria was whimpering on the sofa. He stopped when he saw I was dressed in the captain's uniform, then made a few interrogative noises. I watched him a moment and asked, "How come you have everyone at the mine at the same time?"

He made noises through two pairs of socks.

I tried a couple of doors that led off the office. One led to a boardroom, and another led to a small kitchen. The third led to a luxurious bathroom, and there, as I expected, I found a first aid kit. I took it to where Santa Maria was lying and extracted the bandage roll. I showed him the plum-sized piece of C4 and pressed a detonator into it.

"This is C4 plastic explosive, Santa Maria. This amount will blow a two-inch steel bar in half. So you can imagine what it will do to your spinal cord and chest."

I pressed it onto his back and taped it there firmly with a lot of tape. When I was done, I sat him up and put more tape all the way around his chest, securing it in place. Finally I showed him my cell.

"The detonator is connected to my phone. When I dial the appropriate number, it blows. Now let's be clear, Santa Maria, I want you alive and testifying before Congress. So I will be reluctant to dial that number. But if you twitch at the wrong time, breathe too deeply when we pass one of your soldiers, or walk just a little too fast, I will blow you in half. Do you understand me so far?"

He nodded and made more noises.

"We are going to walk out of here. You will be dressed normally, and you will act normally. We will get in my car, and we will leave. So—" I took the socks out of his mouth, and he gasped for air.

"My heart! I'm going to have a heart attack!"

"Shut up."

He closed his mouth and made rasping noises. I went on.

"How come you have everyone at the mine at the same time, instead of working twenty-four-seven in shifts?"

"Using light at night makes us too visible from the sky and satellites. And we are well ahead of schedule. Better they rest at night."

I nodded. It made sense.

"OK, when we get to the gate, what happens? What do you have to show them?"

"My face. My face is enough."

"High tech."

"Just me and Drake. Everybody else..."

"But I'm with you so we get through, right?"

"Yes."

I cut his bonds. "Get dressed. Fast."

I went to the desk, grabbed the hard drive, the laptop, and any flash drives I could find, and carried them to the door. I opened it and spoke to the soldiers. "You two, take these down to my Jeep. It's parked right outside, and it's open. Put them in back and head over to hangar 18. Wait there."

"Yes, sir!"

They grabbed the stuff and hurried down. I went back inside. Santa Maria was gaping. He still had his pants around his knees.

"Get cracking," I told him. "You don't want to be here in ten minutes."

He dragged on his pants, his Italian slip-on shoes, and his jacket and hurried out of the office to wait for the elevator. I showed him the cell.

"Slow down, stay close, and be cool."

He nodded, and his hands did a little dance like he was trying to find a way to reach between his shoulder blades.

"Be cool," I said again, and he did some more nodding. We rode down to the lobby. By now it was busy, and we crossed it, dodging a few people. A couple nodded and smiled at Santa Maria. He was sweating a lot and ignored everybody, but nobody seemed to notice.

We got out to the parking lot, and I opened the passenger door for him. He climbed in, and I went around and got behind the wheel. I fired up the big engine and reversed out, then moved calmly and steadily toward the main gate. Santa Maria said, "I think I'm having a heart attack."

"Not before we're through the gates, you're not."

"You animal, you are subhuman."

"That's what my dad said when I was born. Then he added, 'You take after your mother.'"

He boggled at me. "How can you, at a time like this?"

"Relax, we're coming to the gate."

We pulled up, and a soldier came over. He peered through the window, and his eyes said he recognized me from when I came in.

"Captain?" he said it as a question, like he was inviting me to explain why I was wearing the uniform. I arched an eyebrow at him. "What is it, Corporal?"

"When I saw you before, sir, you weren't in uniform."

I gave a small nod, more like he had confirmed my impression of his IQ than agreeing with him. "Thank you. I had noticed the same thing. Was there anything else? Mr. Santa Maria would like to get to his destination."

He looked past me at the man with the C4 taped to his back and frowned. "I'm sorry, sir, are you OK? Do you need a medic?"

I looked at Santa Maria. He looked like a man who is pretending not to be having a heart attack. "I'm fine!" he snapped. "Just open the damned gate!"

"Yes, sir."

He stepped over to his booth, and the door began to roll open. We eased through, and I began to accelerate. "Did you know," I said, as I pulled my cell fro my jacket, "that lithium is highly explosive when subjected to intense heat?"

His expression was one of really not wanting to know what I was talking about. At a quarter of a mile out, I slowed and flipped to the number pad with my thumb. Then I stopped and pressed number nine.

The explosions were bigger than even I had expected. We

were a quarter of a mile from the base and almost half a mile from the warehouses, but the blast and the shockwave lifted the trunk of the Jeep and drove it forward at least six feet. Santa Maria screamed, ducked, and covered his head. In the rearview mirror, I saw a massive fireball rise like a mushroom cloud into the air. I turned in my seat and stared through the rear window. The row of hangars containing number 23 took the brunt of the blast, and I knew what would come next. I pressed eight on my cell, and the remaining C4 in the prefab at the mine exploded. I prayed to whatever gods would listen to me that the slaves in the mine would get the message, if they hadn't gotten it already.

I climbed out and stood staring. The entire sky was on fire. I could see people, frantic stencils against the furious glow of the eruption, running wildly this way and that. Some were on fire.

I could see now that the fire was engulfing hangar 23, and I scrambled back into the Jeep. Santa Maria was goggling at me. "*What have you done? What have you done?*"

"Done? I'm not done yet, you son of a bitch. I still have lots of work to do!"

I floored the pedal, and we roared out of there, bathed in the broiling light that was dimming the sun. A moment later, there was another explosion, where the intense heat had gotten to the batteries and ignited them. I skidded and turned across the road so I could look back. I saw the massive, combined balls of fire swarm across the complex, towering over the guard towers in the camp, consuming them and erupting through the steel wall and the razor wire perimeter. It tore the whole place to pieces and hurled debris high into the air. Black smoke billowed across the sky and hid the sun until it was almost as black as night.

I spun the wheel and started back for Es Arenal.

Only, when I got there, instead of turning in through the fields where I had found Maisy Middleton, I kept going, on up the road toward South Faro, where the Temple and the satellite dish were. Santa Maria seemed to freeze in his seat. After a while, he asked in a strange voice, "What are you doing?"

"I'm not sure, Santa Maria. Why don't you tell me? What am I doing?"

He turned what should have been a smile into a horrible, twisted grimace. "Strange question," he said. "Where are you taking me?"

"Same answer." I glanced at him. "Where am I taking you?"

"Riddles..."

"Yeah, right? Riddles."

It wasn't a long drive. Nowhere was very far on that island. We were soon climbing through the red, rocky landscape, heading for the eerie form of the Temple, stark against the pale sky.

"Why..." His voice was a rasp.

I nodded. "Yeah, why?"

A couple of minutes later, I pulled up outside the huge oak doors in the shadow of the vast dish aerial. The doors were open wide, but nothing was visible in the darkness inside. I climbed down from the Jeep. I opened the rear passenger door, pulled the X95 and the P226 from my rucksack, and moved around to Santa Maria. He was sitting, staring through the glass at me. I opened the door.

"Get out."

"But why? What do we want here? You said Washington."

"Are you going to get out, or do I have to drag you out?"

"Animal."

He said it with no special inflection. He climbed down, and I pushed him gently toward the Temple. We climbed the stairs, and at the doors he stopped, and his voice came out as a strange, high-pitched wine, a long, almost wailing "No..."

I put my hand on his back and spoke close to his ear. "You ride with the devil, Joseph, you end up getting burned."

I shoved harder, and he stumbled across the threshold. I went after him, and at the end of the nave, standing in front of the altar, was Father João da Silva. With the long, narrow perspective, he looked strangely tall. I couldn't see the features of his face in the half-light, and his voice seemed to echo out of the air itself.

"You are Satan? You are here to try and stop us?"

Santa Maria was weeping, with his head hung low. He was muttering, "Father, forgive me. I have been weak. Forgive me, Father. We were taken by surprise."

When we got to the priest, Santa Maria got on his knees before da Silva and sank forward with his head on the floor at the priest's feet.

"Father, we thought we had him. He was our prisoner. He twisted things, he manipulated... I don't know how..."

Father da Silva looked down at him, and his face twisted with disgust.

"Shut up, Santa Maria. I will deal with you later." He raised his eyes to meet mine. "Who are you and what do you want?"

"I am Harry Bauer, and I want revenge. I am Maisy Middleton. I am Sally Haight. I am Madeleine Vasco. I am countless other children whose ghosts stand behind me, demanding justice, and I am Harry Bauer, their avenger. I want blood."

"You are insane."

"You better believe it, Father. Now I am going to ask both

of you, who killed Maisy Middleton, Sally Haight, and Madeleine Vasco?"

Da Silva's face seemed to congeal into a mask of complacent intransigence. Santa Maria's weeping was becoming convulsive. I took a step back, pulled my Sig, and shot him through the knee. His scream was horrific. It echoed against the walls and reverberated in the ceiling. Da Silva stepped back and averted his face.

I said, "You think I won't do that to you? Who killed the girls?"

Santa Maria was screaming and sobbing by turns, "Tell him! Tell him, for God's sake!" I wanted to feel pity for him, but all I could see was the slave laborers in the pit, the children, and Maisy's dead corpse in my arms.

"That is not for you to know. You think I am scared of you? I am protected by a greater power than you can comprehend."

I nodded. "Sure. You're dangerous, and I'm out of my mind. You have your specs on upside down, Father."

He snorted. "There was no one to protect the village."

"Jesus! Does nobody talk straight on this island? Does everybody tell you some weird story when you ask them a question? Who killed those girls?"

"Do not utter that name in this house. You asked me a question. I am answering you. You went to wreak havoc on the only industry on this island"—he smiled—"and you left that poor village of Es Arenal unprotected. It was not difficult for me, a man of the cloth, the island's longstanding, trusted spiritual guide, to go down and find some assistants for the afternoon. They are not usually willing. You know children can be awkward, but they are always amenable to a little persuasion, if not with money and candy, then with a whip."

I felt the hot burn of panic in my belly. "What are you talking about?"

"I am talking about the reason you will not kill Mr. Santa Maria. I am talking about the reason you will not kill me." He leaned forward and gave me a disturbing, reptilian smile. "I am talking about the reason you will lay down your weapons and surrender your animalistic self to me, you disgusting brute."

He turned his head toward the transept and bellowed, "Julian! Bring the girls! And bring some first aid—" He waved a hand at Santa Maria. "A tourniquet or something."

I heard the creak of unoiled hinges and the shuffle of bare feet. It was an altar boy in his red and gold with his blue cap. I had seen him before. He was one of those twelve akolouthos who had sat with Maisy. His face was hideously disfigured, but he was tall and very strongly built. In his hand he had a rope with which he was leading five young girls. They could not have been more than fourteen or fifteen years old. Each was dressed in a sack which had holes cut for the neck and the arms. The rope was tied around each of their necks. They were all weeping.

He led them in front of the altar and sat on the altar steps, where he was hidden from view behind the girls. Another altar boy came scurrying out after them. He was the one with a single eye. He too was big and strongly built. In his hand he carried a first aid box, some rope, and a stick. As he set to work on Santa Maria's leg, Father da Silva began to speak.

"Julian has a knife. It is very long, very slender, and very, very sharp. If I tell him to, he will drive that knife into some part of one of the girls' anatomy. Maybe it will be fatal. Maybe it won't. Maybe it will just be very, very painful. He is very simple. He is not a physician. He just likes stabbing girls. You understand? Or he might cut one. We never really know what

Julian is going to do next." He gave a small laugh. "As far as I can see, you have two ways of saving these girls from what will become intolerable pain and suffering. You can kill Julian, or you can do exactly as I say." He grinned his horrific, reptilian grin and gestured at the line of girls. "But of course, Julian is out of sight! What to do? It seems, Mr. Bauer, I have you!"

SIXTEEN

My eyes connected with the girl who was standing directly in front of Julian. She was staring hard at me, like she was trying to send some kind of telepathic message. I looked at da Silva.

"Don't hurt the girls. I'll do whatever you tell me, but let the girls go. This is between you and me. They are no part of it. What do you want?"

He hunched his shoulder and chuckled. "You feel you are in a position to make demands, Bauer? Let me tell you there is exactly nothing to stop me killing you and the girls, and there is damned all you can do about it."

"Deny me the hope that I can save the girls, Father, and I'll blow your brains all over your damned temple."

"Fair point. So let's start by you laying down your weapon."

"And Julian lays down his knife."

His smile was deliberate, to let me know he was lying. He was enjoying his game. He nodded. "Yes, quite, but you first, Mr. Bauer."

I fixed the girl with my eyes. She held my gaze and blinked once. I held up the Sig for him to see and said, "OK, I'm laying it down." I bent forward, extending my right leg behind me, and glanced up at the girl.

It hadn't been telepathy. It had been shared common sense and resourcefulness. She spread her legs wide, and I dropped on my belly and took the shot of my life. I fired twice in rapid succession. The bullets zapped between her knees and struck Julian in the lower belly. He let out a horrific howl and tried to get to his feet, clawing at his wounds. I didn't waste time watching him. I rolled on my left side and fired at the father. He was running toward Julian, but the slug caught him in the side and hurled him to the floor.

I sensed rather than heard the movement behind me and rolled on my back as the kid with one eyed loomed over me holding the stick for Santa Maria's tourniquet like a spear. I shot him twice in his only eye. His brains erupted out the back of his head and sprayed all over the governor, who started to scream.

I was on my feet and running. The girls were stirring and milling, still tied at the neck. I skidded past them, noting that da Silva was still alive, squirming on the floor. Julian was on his back, crying and groaning. I felt bad about him and One-Eye, but I'd had no choice. I put him out of his misery, telling myself there were ten more of these characters and I needed to be quick.

I snapped, "Don't move!" and the girls froze. I picked up Julian's knife and made four cuts in the rope. I pointed to the door. "There is a Jeep outside. Go to it and get in. Lock the doors and let nobody in unless it's me. *Go!*"

They ran. I turned to Father da Silva. "Give me one good reason not to execute you right here and now."

He was clutching at his side. From what I could see, it was a through and through that had clipped his left lung low down. With medical help he'd live. Without it, he'd either bleed out or drown in his own blood.

"Who the hell are you?" He was speaking between painful gasps. "Who do you represent?"

I curled my lip. "Humanity."

I raised the gun and took aim at his head. He held up his hands, like he could ward off the bullet. "Wait!"

"For what?"

"I can…" He swallowed and took a breath, looking around him like he was desperately searching for whatever it was he could do. "I can…" and suddenly he was screaming, "*Come to me! Come to me, akolouthos! Akolouthos! Come to me!*"

"Son of a bitch!" I raised my weapon to shoot, but behind me, I heard the oak door smash open. On my right, I could hear Santa Maria wailing again. And Father da Silva was now bellowing, "*Kill, akolouthos! Kill! Kill! Kill! Kill, akolouthos!*"

I looked behind me, and all ten of them in their red robes with golden sashes were lumbering around the altar from the vestry. I ran, grabbed Santa Maria by the scruff of his neck, and yelled at him, "*Run! Run!*"

But they were fast, and they were not carrying a guy with no knee. They were on us before we had taken four strides. Behind them, da Silva was still screaming "*Kill! Kill! Kill!*"

They swarmed over da Silva, dragging him to the floor, pummeling and beating him, and pretty soon they had knives out, and it was ugly. I hesitated a couple of seconds, but when a couple of them started after me, I beat it fast toward the truck, bellowing, "*Open the driver's door! Open it!*"

As I ran, with them grunting and lumbering behind me, I could see the girls through the windshield. They were immobile, paralyzed with fear, staring at me. I gestured frantically as I ran, screaming, "*Open the damned door! Open the door!*"

I scrambled around the hood, pulling the Sig from my belt. As I reached for the handle, the hulk was just six feet behind me and closing fast. I had no time to grab the door. I shoved the Sig in his face and pulled the trigger twice. As he staggered back, he collided with two of his pals. I grabbed the handle of the door and pulled. It was locked. I rapped on the glass, screaming at them to open.

The hulk hit the ground. The two behind him struggled with each other to climb over him, reaching for me with huge, powerful hands. I hammered on the glass, aimed at them and pulled the trigger, and heard the sickly click click of the empty magazine. The hulks lunged at me. I stepped back, and in my peripheral vision, I saw a screaming girl reach across and open the lock. A hand grabbed my face as the door opened an inch. I grabbed the door with both hands, and with a strength born of terror, I smashed that door into the brute's face, not once but three times. Then I clambered in, slammed the door closed, and fired up the engine as eight of the poor bastards hurled themselves at the truck, the doors, and the windows.

I floored the pedal and reversed. The tires screamed, and four of da Silva's monsters stumbled and fell to the road. I spun the wheel, rammed in first, second, and third and accelerated fast on the road back toward Es Arenal.

My mind was racing as I drove. Had I done it? They were all dead, except da Silva, but he was badly hurt, and I could go back for him. Either way, even if he survived, which was doubtful, the operation was destroyed. My next steps were to get these kids home, then call the brigadier, finish off da Silva if I could, and get myself off the damned island.

As we hurtled east and north along the road, I could see

black clouds building in the north, over the ocean. I allowed myself a grim smile. They would find plenty of bodies in the next rainstorm, but none of them would be children. They would be the bodies of those who preyed on the children. An eye for an eye, a life for a life.

As we turned in and approached the town, I glanced at the girl in the front passenger seat.

"What's your name?"

"Miriam."

I looked at her again. Less of a glance this time. She was about fourteen, with dark hair and dark eyes. Synchronicity, I told myself. "You saved my life. Thank you."

"You saved ours. We panicked a bit, but I knew I couldn't let them get you."

I smiled, watching the road as I slowed to enter the square. "Back atcha. Tell me where to go. Who gets out first?"

"Sandra and Corinne are neighbors. They're on the right, the first corner on Middle Street." She was silent as I drove past the Sea Breeze, then added. "It's horrible what they do if they catch you."

We watched Sandra and Corinne run to their doors and hammer and ring the bells. We watched the parents come out, and there was a lot of hugging and weeping.

"Who's next?"

Miriam looked over her shoulder. "Carmen is at the end of Middle Street, on the right, on Meadow Lane. Then Ciara, and then me. We are both on Mill Walk, but I am farther down."

I took off, following the route she had told me.

"Who are those kids? The ones with the deformed heads?"

"May God forgive me." She said it quietly. "It would have been better if you had killed them all."

I was astonished and let my face say so when I stared at her.

"They were just children. They didn't know what they were doing. They have some kind of disease."

"No." She shook her head, looking down at her hands. "We don't know who they are, or where they come from, but there are rumors. Sometimes the soldiers come to the bars, and they drink too much and they talk. These...*monsters*, they are not children. Father da Silva cares for them, but they come from the Company. They force the workers to breed, and they take the children and they do things to them, to their brains."

"Do things? Like what?"

One of the girls spoke up from the back. "Miriam! We are not supposed to talk about this!"

Her face flushed with anger, and she half turned, snapping over her shoulder, "How long do we continue in silence? And what for? To keep safe? Is that what we are? Safe? We are as safe as sheep at a slaughter house! Didn't you see? The governor is dead! Three of the akolouthos are dead! You *heard* the explosion! You *saw* the fire! Must we live with the fear forever? Even after the danger has passed?"

The voice from the back became tremulous. "You don't know."

I turned into Meadow Lane, and Miriam pointed to a house about halfway along. As I pulled up, I said, "Drake and Santa Maria are dead. The mine and the Company are completely destroyed. Sheriff Jeremiah Scott and his deputies are dead. The prisoners at the mine are free."

I heard the door in back open and slam closed. A moment later, I saw one of the girls running to the cottage Miriam had pointed to. The door opened, and a couple ran out and embraced her, hugging her close. I moved on.

After a moment, Miriam said, "We don't know anything for certain. Maybe the soldiers were lying. But they said there was a laboratory at the plant, and they were experimenting with human brains. They wanted to adapt young children's brains so that they would grow to be part of a machine, or machines, like the computers on board a plane or a drone. They wanted to alter them so that they would be violent and aggressive in nature, so they could be part of weapons."

"And those poor kids were the failed experiments."

"I suppose so, if the soldiers were telling the truth." I sighed as I turned into Mill Walk, and she pointed to a cute house on the right. "That's Ciara's place there."

I pulled up and heard the door open. There was a pause, and then her voice came softly. "Thank you, Mr. Bauer."

"You got it, kid."

We watched and made sure she was safely with her parents and moved on a couple of hundred yards to a slightly bigger house.

She put her hand on the handle and hesitated a moment. "I'd ask you to come in and meet my parents. They'll want to thank you. But my father was beaten quite badly when he tried to stop them taking me."

"He's a brave man. You take after him."

She smiled. "He tries to teach us that it's our duty to our family and our people to fight to protect ourselves. We are a very small minority. We don't belong to the congregation, and Father da Silva has always been hostile to my father. So has the governor."

"I figured. Is your dad the rabbi?"

She smiled, then gave a small laugh. "Yes, he's the rabbi." She reached over and gave me a kiss on the cheek. "Thank you, Mr. Bauer."

"Harry. I won't say it was a pleasure, but it was an honor."

I watched her run down the path and hammer on the door.

It opened, and a woman and a man fought each other to get out. The three of them clung to each other, weeping while Miriam babbled and pointed at the Jeep. The man raised his hand to me. I raised mine back, though I doubt he saw because the sky was growing dark. I hit the horn a couple of short jabs and pulled away.

I made my way back toward the town square. When I arrived, I saw there was a light on in one of the top windows at City Hall. I thought about going up and giving the mayor a severe case of what the brigadier would call defenestration but decided his involvement had probably been minimal and the brigadier might have some use for him. Instead I pulled my cell from my jacket, saw I had signal, and called the office.

"Universal Solutions, how may I direct your call?"

"This is Harry Bauer. I need to talk to the boss."

There was a pause while she checked voice recognition. Then she said, "Putting you through."

A moment later, the brigadier voice snapped, "Harry."

"Did you pick it up?"

"Yes, we were about to move in."

"I left the mayor for you, and there's a priest called Father João da Silva. He's hurt, but he's alive, and he was an important part of the cabal. I think you need to talk to him."

"Are you all right?"

"Yeah. I need to get off this island, but there is a big storm coming. Sir?"

"Yes, Harry."

"I don't know what strings you can pull, but the people on this island need protection."

"I understand. We're on our way. Where are you?"

"The hotel at Es Arenal. The St. Homer, or I-Takka, take your pick."

"Sit tight."

He hung up, and I climbed down from the truck, feeling suddenly weary, and made my way into the hotel, wondering if I could find some food and a drink. But before that I found Doctor Caroline Brown. I saw her through the arch into the dining room. She was sitting where I had sat the day I stole her yacht. She had an ashtray and a bottle of Bells Scotch whisky on the table in front of her. I went and leaned on the wall, looking down at her. We held each other's eye for a moment before she said, "Pull up a glass and sit down."

SEVENTEEN

I PUSHED OFF THE WALL AND WENT AND SAT AT HER table. I took one of the wine glasses from the setting and poured an inch of whisky into it, then pulled off half. I set the glass down and closed my eyes.

Her voice cut into the peaceful darkness.

"Hard day at the office, dear?"

I opened one eye enough to raise a brow at her. "Yeah, it was a hard day at the office."

She looked down at her glass. "They came and took Marguerite and Camilla. There was nothing I could do to stop them."

"I know."

She watched me, waiting for me to explain. I didn't bother. Finally she said, "There was an explosion."

"There were two."

"What have you done, Harry?"

I took another pull on the whisky. It was fierce, but it helped.

"I killed everybody." I surprised myself at the pain I felt

inside on speaking those words. She narrowed her eyes and frowned. "*You did what?*"

"That's an exaggeration. I didn't kill you, and I didn't kill the mayor. And I only nearly killed da Silva. But I killed everybody else. I killed Drake, I killed Captain Nick Wise, I killed a hundred or two guys whose names I don't know. I killed three of the akolouthos, and I allowed about ten of them to kill the governor." I watched her face for a long moment. It was expressionless, watching me back. "The explosions you heard. I improvised a bomb that fed off the tons of lithium they had there. It was bigger than even I expected. A gigantic fireball. It engulfed the whole camp. I've seen my share of explosions, but I'd never seen anything like that."

A small frown contracted her brow. "The workers..."

I felt suddenly weak, exhausted. I felt as if my soul was draining away. I reached for the bottle and poured myself another shot. Before knocking it back, I said, "They were at the mine. I killed the guards and the truck drivers. They were still in the mine when the place blew."

When she spoke, it was little more than a whisper. "My God... what are you?"

"What am I? It's a good question. I guess I'm an avenging angel. Is revenge God's job? Or does he delegate that to the devil? Maybe I'm the devil's handyman, Satan's instrument of vengeance."

"Stop it."

A cold breeze touched me. I said, "I need to go and pack my bag. I have to get out of here."

She gave a small shake of her head. "You're not going anywhere in this." She pointed past me, and I turned to look. It was as dark as early evening. Absently I said, "Your yacht is still at Sandy Cove."

"No," she said. I looked back at her. "I am not letting you take it to Surinam or Guyana. In this storm you'll sink it, and you will drown. I don't want either of those things to happen."

As she said it, the patter started, soft at first but growing stronger. I turned back, put my elbows on the table, and rubbed my face. I kept getting flashes in my mind of the vast fireball engulfing the plant. How many people were there in it? A hundred? Two hundred? What were their names? Where did they go to school? Were they in love? Did they have children? How many of them were directly responsible for the slavery there?

And then the grotesque, deformed faces of the akolouthos thrust toward me out of the flames. I pulled the trigger, and they exploded in blood and gore.

"Hey!"

I opened my eyes.

"You're quite something, huh?"

"I'm a killer."

"You killed them all. You destroyed the Company, you discovered the akolouthos—"

"You knew about them."

"Of course I did. I'm the only doctor on the island. When those kids came out of the lab, they needed looking after. A lot of them died."

"Did you know it was them killing the girls?"

She didn't answer right away. Then she gave a snort and something that wanted to be a smile but was too sad. "Why do you think I smoke and drink too much? I suspected. Those kids were taken from their mothers at birth. They were fed on rich protein drinks and subjected to experiments on their brains."

"Why the mutations?"

"Some of them were mutations but not all of them. They worked on them while they were still in the womb and fed the mothers experimental drugs. The objective was to develop a brain that would be responsive to transplant in an environment where it could develop an organic interface with AI. Of course they were starting from scratch. That's why they needed a place like this, outside of anybody's jurisdiction."

"Sweet Jesus." I stared into my drink. "You said some of them were experiments..."

"The others were subjected to invasive surgery, sometimes without anesthetic, to see how the nerve tissue would react to certain implants. If it would reject them or attach."

"Did you—"

"No! There's a limit, Harry. I'm no hero, or heroine. I am not brave enough to stand up to those bastards and fight them. I haven't got the body or the spirit for it. But there is a limit beyond which I will not go. They had their own scientists conducting the experiments. They didn't need a second-rate doctor, and I would not have done it anyway." She sighed and said with more feeling than I would have expected, "There comes a point when life isn't worth staying alive for."

Then she raised her face and studied mine. "You got here just before it reached that point. We should be grateful."

I studied her back and almost made it to a smile. "I'm glad I could oblige. I may have crossed that line today."

She stood and came around the table. She stood close and ran her fingers through my hair. She smelled strongly of whisky and tobacco, but somehow it was good. In that moment, it smelled honest and real.

"Hey, Harry, you killed a lot of very bad people. There was no one at that plant who wasn't a party to those atrocities. They were all very dark, evil people. And you have given a lot of good people a chance at life, a chance to be free. The world doesn't like men like you, but the world needs men like you." She gave a rueful smile, bent down, and gave me an oddly intoxicating kiss, strong with the flavor of Camel cigarettes and whisky. When she pulled back, she smiled and said, "Whatever the world may think, I like you."

I didn't answer. I couldn't. She placed her hand on my cheek. The rain lashed hard at the window, and the wind rattled the door of the hotel.

"Now what do you say," she said, "to a steak and my special olive oil fries, a bottle of wine, and a nice cuddle in bed until the storm passes? Then we can go and get my yacht, and you can get me off this damned island and take me to Guyana."

"It sounds like I died and went to paradise."

A smile that was more sad than amused crawled up her right cheek. "Let's take it one step at a time, tough guy. I'm no angel. I'm just a doctor who does what she can to help people who are sick."

And she turned and made her way to the kitchen.

It was raining. It seemed it had always been raining. It was dark, and the cool smell of wet earth crept in through the open window on a listless breeze. I didn't know how long I had slept. I had awoken gradually to the splash and drip of the rain.

I reached for the doc but found only cool sheets. Across the room I saw the thin strip of light under the door.

I wondered vaguely what time it was and whether the brigadier's men had arrived. Was that why the doc had gotten up? But if so, she would have called me.

Or not: just a doctor who does what she can to help people who are sick.

I sat up and made my way to the bathroom, where I stepped under a cold shower, washed my hair and my body, went hot and cold again, toweled myself dry, shaved and dressed. Then I sat on the end of the bed and pulled my phone from my jacket, intending to call the brigadier and see where he was at.

I had no signal.

I stood, put the Sig under my arm, pulled on my jacket, slipped the fighting knife in my boot, and stepped out into the corridor.

Maybe the destruction of the facility at the mine had damaged the telephone system. Maybe it hadn't. I walked quietly to the top of the stairs and listened. There was no sound from downstairs.

I crossed to the far side of the stairs so I could see the entrance to the reception, the entrance to the dining room, and part of the corridor that ran under the landing. There was no one there waiting to shoot me.

I slipped the Sig from under my arm and went down the stairs. There was no one there. I could still hear nothing. I went into the dining room.

They were sitting at the far end. They had pulled two tables together. Father João da Silva was in the middle, facing me across the table. He looked very pale, slightly yellow, and he was sweating. He probably had a fever. There were eight of his akolouthos sitting four on either side of him, each more hideous and grotesque than the last. At the far left was the doc, Caroline. She didn't look at me. She seemed to be making a minute examination of the tablecloth. His followers sat in what looked like a vegetative state, waiting for his instructions to eat somebody. But him? He was watching me, despite his fever, with black rage in his eyes.

"We were just going to go and get you," he said.

"The prophet and his acolytes." I pointed at them. "This is the best you can do? Not exactly Buddha or Jesus Christ, is it? Hell, it's not even Rajneesh and his ninety-three Rolls Royce. Your disciples were twelve failed experiments on an island nobody wanted. Way to go, da Silva."

I glanced at the doc. "You patch him up?"

"I'm a doctor."

"Right," I said with more bitterness than I expected. "You sure know your medicine."

She closed her eyes, but that was the extent of her reaction. Da Silva ignored the exchange and continued, "I am going to kill you, Mr. Bauer. There is nothing you can do to avoid it. I want nothing from you, I don't give a damn who you are or whom you work for. You have made all that irrelevant. All I want is your death."

"But you're still talking."

"Yes because your death in itself is not enough. You may scorn our Temple and my akolouthos, but our faith is true, and I know there is an afterlife. I know our souls live on and carry with them the experiences of this life. And when you pass, when my akolouthos kill and eat you, not necessarily in that order, I want you to *know* exactly what you have done and how badly you have harmed the world and humanity."

I was looking at them, calibrating them, working out how many I could take out before they got to me. If they had been ordinary men, sitting as they were behind a table that stood between me and them, I might have taken them all. Take out the two at the far ends, and they would form obstacles for the remaining six. Trapped behind the table they'd be sitting ducks.

But these were not ordinary men. I had seen them in a frenzy, and they would swarm over and around the table at speed, trampling over their fallen colleagues. I might take out three or four, but once the remaining four or five got me, it would be curtains—and very unpleasant curtains at that.

"I'm a slow learner," I said. "Ask the doc. She's taught me the same lesson three times over, and I still get it wrong. But go ahead, explain to me how liberating slaves, the subjects of human experiments that turn babies into monsters, has harmed humanity. Tell me how destroying a mining enterprise that used slave labor and child slaves harmed the world and humanity. I'm listening, da Silva, so I can take that information with me to hell when you murder me."

He looked real ill, as though he was in pain, but he curled his lip and sneered, "Spare me your schoolgirl morality. Where were your morals when you murdered Mohammed Ben Amini?[1] You were not so troubled by morality then, were you? Yes, I have researched you, and I know all about you."

"He was like you. He had no trouble murdering and torturing kids, women, men, the old, and the vulnerable. It was all the same to him. So I had no problem killing him like I'll have no problem killing you."

"You are blinded by your own stupidity, Bauer. In twenty years, Europe and Britain will be Islamic states. Maybe even parts of the United States. They are accruing power on every level, politically, economically, militarily, *culturally*, and all the while their evil servants are spreading throughout the Western World, playing our conscience, accusing us of racism, playing the ethnic victim card, exploiting the Universal Declaration of Human rights to implant their evil *metastasis* around the globe

1. See *Dead of Night*

to fulfill Mohammed's aim to convert the whole of humanity to Islam—subjugation!"

"And you aim to stop them by using slave labor."

His face flushed, and he half-screamed, "*Open your eyes, for God's sake! Can you not see what's happening?*" He took a handkerchief and mopped his face. Caroline was watching him closely. He went on, "Iran is a few months from completing a hypersonic nuclear missile. And Trump's peace plan has ensured that Hamas retains their place inside Israel. Russia, while keeping the world focused in Ukraine, is actively assisting Iran in its nuclear development. Spain is leaving NATO and actively embracing its Arab past, Paris, Berlin, Brussels, Amsterdam, Oslo, London, New York, DC, San Francisco, Los Angeles, Huston and Austin, and hundreds more cities in the Western World have huge Islamic populations who are insinuating themselves into positions of political power at every level of society. And jihad, that they are entitled to kill and enslave anyone who refuses to convert, is the central tenet of their grotesque ideology."

I drew breath, but he cut across me. "We are running out of time. We are in a race against an existential threat. Everything we have fought to achieve over the last five hundred years is about to be taken from us. And we are passively allowing it to happen. Why? Because our democratically elected leaders live from election to election, and to confront the dangers of Islam, to offend Islamic voters and pressure groups, is to risk losing votes."

"You enslaved people and experimented on the brains of living children!"

"And that was wrong. But allowing China and Russia to get ahead of us and share that technology with Islamic leaders would be worse. Now after what you have done, you have ensured the rise to power of a universal Islamic Sharia world order."

I said, "You're full of bullshit," but it lacked conviction, and he seemed not to hear me.

"Nobody knows better than you, Bauer, that in war you have to make sacrifices, and sometimes those sacrifices are hard to swallow. The surgical strike is a myth. You know that and I know that. Those slaves, as you call them, and the experiments, were essential. We are at war. We have been at war for millennia. At war with *Evil!* What do you do when your enemy is developing advanced weapons and your only chance of getting ahead of him is to take actions that are morally reprehensible? What do you do when refusing to take that action means the extinction of Western civilization? Can you answer that?"

"No." I shook my head. "But nothing excuses what you did, whatever the price we have to pay. If we find ourselves experimenting on living babies' brains, the Evil has already won."

He scowled at me and snarled, "Kill him, eat him!"

EIGHTEEN

THEY CAME LIKE THE STAMPEDE I HAD EXPECTED. MY first shot hit the akolouthos on my far left, next to the dock. It hit him in the center of the forehead, and the doc started to scream. I had that corner jammed for at least four seconds. My second hit the guy on the far right square in the heart. He stood gaping at me, blocking the way for the three guys next to him.

In that moment, the plan I had which was making the gods piss their robes laughing was to pick off the six akolouthos logjammed in the middle before taking out Father João da Silva, Defender of Democracy and Human Rights.

The gods laughed, and da Silva's acolytes, as if of a single mind, hurled the two tables across the dining room at me and charged. I backed up, firing, and hit one of them in the chest, but they were fast, and before I could get off a third round, they were on me. One seized my left hand by the wrist and my upper arm. Another on my right grabbed the Sig with one hand and my right wrist with the other. The one on my left, with crazed eyes, opened his mouth wide and, with terrifying strength, dragged my arm up toward his teeth.

I struggled frantically to resist, but his strength was enormous. The guy on my right was prying the Sig from my hand. I pulled the trigger twice without aiming. He screamed like a dinosaur with a mad hornet up its ass and let go. I didn't think; I smashed the butt of the Sig into the other guy's face, aiming for his twisted, lopsided eyes. But the other three were already on me, stumbling over their pals, all now screaming and reaching for me like something out of a crazy zombie movie.

I backed up, firing two more rounds into their midst that seemed to do nothing and scrambled through the arch, heading for the stairs. It was high ground they could only climb one at a time—two with difficulty. The gods were still laughing.

They stampeded out through the arch and ran for the stairs. Two started to climb, and the other three, a couple of whom were bleeding, took hold of the banisters and ripped them off. I pulled off one shot, maybe two, but hands grabbed my legs, my arm, and my clothes and dragged me down to the floor. And then they were on top of me in a frenzy, punching, kicking, stamping. I felt teeth sink into my left arm.

It was a fraction of a second, but I remembered reading that in moments like that, if you think about what's happening to you, you die. The only way to survive is to focus your mind on your weapon and use it. I roared like a demented beast to block out all my thoughts but one. I pilled up my right knee and pulled my Fairbairn and Sykes from my boot and went to work. I stabbed and slashed at everything and anything I could find: a belly, a chest, a leg, a face descending on my arm again. And as I stabbed and slashed, I kicked and thrashed too, scrambling my way out from underneath them.

There was a lot of blood pooling on the floor, and as I staggered to my feet, I saw one of them was on his knees, bleeding profusely from his belly. The others looked like the pain from multiple knife and gunshot wounds was getting to them. For half a second, my instinct was to charge and kill as many as I could before retreating and regrouping.

But a second look at them told me they were more frenzied than they were in pain. I shoved the knife into my boot, and as they charged, I made for the dining room again. My backup plan was to use da Silva as a hostage. Outside, the sky rumbled with more divine laughter.

I charged through the arch and saw he had anticipated me and had a semi-automatic in his hands. He watched me with baleful eyes.

My left arm was in severe pain from the bites, and I could feel warm blood oozing onto my hand. As the akolouthos charged through the arch, I turned and ran into that area of the hotel I had never been in before. It turned out to be the bar, and it was in darkness. Without thinking, I ran behind the counter with massive, powerful hands pulling at my jacket. Right next to me, by the cash register, there was a two-thirds full bottle of scotch. I grabbed it by the neck with my left hand and, screaming in pain, I turned and smashed it against the brute's head. Whisky flooded over him, and he stopped in his tracks. I didn't pause. I rammed the jagged glass into his throat.

Then my eye caught a small, black disposable lighter beside a corkscrew in a white saucer. And as the beast choked and staggered back, I reached out and flicked the flint. He went up in blue flames, screaming and walking backward. I pulled the Sig, put two rounds through his head, and snarled, "Now there are just three of you. Now it's a fair fight!"

The three of them were standing, gaping down at their burning brother. I stuck the Sig in my belt and grabbed a bottle of vodka and a bottle of cognac and hurled them, one after another at their feet. A bottle of Famous Grouse followed, and another bottle of vodka. Now there was over a gallon of highly flammable fluid between them and their pal, and it ignited in a big violet and blue whoosh, engulfing the nearest of the three. His inarticulate scream was horrific, but I ignored it and vaulted the bar. I landed among the low, round tables with the Sig in my hand, wondering how many rounds I had left in the magazine.

The two remaining akolouthos charged again. Behind them, their brother, enveloped in flames, was walking in circles waving his arms like some grotesque clockwork toy. The pain in my left hand was so intense I could not use it anymore. I raised the gun one-handed and fired at the nearest hulk. I hit him three times in the chest before he dropped. By that time, his pal was on me. He struck me a tremendous blow across the head. It didn't knock me cold because I managed to weave, but it hurt like hell and sent me reeling. He rushed me as I staggered back, grabbed me, and hurled me like a football across the room, crashing through tables and chairs.

I lay on my back, gasping for air through shards of pain. I looked for the Sig, but it was across the room. Then the monster was on me. He straddled me and let himself drop, landing with his ass on my belly. He must have weighed three hundred pounds, and the pain was excruciating. But the next moment, his huge hands were around my throat, and he was pressing his thumbs into my windpipe. I could see his lips slavering with spittle. His right eye was a grotesque, blind sack. His left eye, too low on his face, goggled at me. I could feel my tongue swelling and my own eyes beginning to bulge as my lungs screamed for air.

For the second time that night I remembered that if you

think about the hands that are strangling you, you will die. Focus your mind on your weapons. Half in spasm and on the edge of darkness, I bent my legs and arched my back so I could pull the fighting knife from my boot. I felt the ridged hilt in my fingers, and with my last glimmer of light before I was engulfed by blackness, I drove the blade deep into his thigh. He bayed like a wounded bull and loosened his grip enough for me to gulp air into my lungs. I didn't waste time feeling sorry for myself. I used that air to roar as I levered the knife back and forth, tore it from his leg and, gripping his left forearm with mine, I slashed deep into his wrist. Blood sprayed out like a hose under pressure, and he struggled, trying to get to his feet. I kicked out from under him and scrambled away, slipping in the growing pool of blood.

I got to my feet and, possessed by a rage that was beyond insanity, I charged him and pounded the knife deep into his fifth intercostal, screaming at him to die.

He went still. The whole world went silent, and he fell with a massive thud onto his back. I stood motionless for what felt like a long time, then turned with a sudden attack of panic, expecting to see Father João da Silva and Dr. Caroline Brown in the arch, holding guns on me. But there was no one there.

I retrieved my gun from the floor and wrenched my knife from the monster's chest. I wiped the blade clean and put it back in my boot. I was having trouble thinking. I told myself my brain had been deprived of oxygen, but I knew I was in shock. Even the SAS doesn't prepare you for being attacked by eight deformed fourteen-year-old monsters who want to eat you, and still you feel guilty about killing them. They are just kids, after all.

Right.

I looked around. The fire had died out behind the bar. I

ejected the magazine from the Sig and checked the ammo. I had half a magazine left, maybe ten rounds.

I walked back to the dining room. They were sitting where I had left them, but they were both looking down at the tablecloth, and da Silva's Glock was lying in front of him. I walked forward a couple of steps.

"How many of these akolouthos did you have?"

He spoke quietly, without looking at me. "Just the twelve you have murdered."

"It's over, da Silva. Everybody is dead except you, the mayor, and the doctor." She looked up at me sharply, like I had surprised her. I ignored it and kept talking. "Give it up. Who is behind this in DC?"

He smiled, still not looking at me, and shook his head. "You are the most destructive human being I have ever met. The death, murder, and mayhem you have caused in less than twenty-four hours is beyond comprehension. I am awed, Mr. Bauer. But even you can not bring down this empire. I have no doubt you will kill me. Maybe you will kill the doctor and Eric, the mayor, though the man is inoffensive." Now he raised his face to look at me. "But Mr. Bauer, we are headed for the stars. We will create paradise on Earth, at last! We are already building a base on the moon, and soon after that is finished, we will start building a base on Mars and start the greening process so that that planet will become habitable once more. And from there we will spread across the solar system, and eventually, as the technology becomes available, we shall spread across the galaxy! We are mighty! You have destroyed this small operation, but believe me, you are insignificant in the greater plan. You are nothing."

"If I am that insignificant, da Silva, you should have no

problem telling me who is behind this project." He said nothing. I turned to the doc. "Do you know?"

She shook her head. I turned back to the priest. "There is one thing keeping you alive right now, da Silva. And that is the possibility that you will name the people behind this project in D.C."

He narrowed his eyes at me. "You are an insignificance, Bauer. We stand in the presence of gods. We fight a war that echoes back through the millennia. We strive for the growth of man. Our angels gave us fire, gave us agriculture, gave us metallurgy, gave us philosophy, so that we could grow to be like them. You want to know who is behind this? I shall tell you. Lucifer, the Bringer of Light! Beelzebub! Belail! Samael! Guardians and protectors of humanity against the Elohim! *That* is who is behind this project, you damned fool! You think you can fight against the gods? Do you think *anything* you can do can stand before them? They are mightier than you can ever imagine!"

"Yeah? If they are so mighty, why do they hide in the shadows and keep their names secret? If they are so mighty, why are you terrified of telling me their names? Why the secrecy?"

He didn't take the bait. He stared at me with contempt, sneered, and said, "It is not the time. I do not need to explain myself to you. They are the highest of the mighty. You are nothing."

It was a pointless exercise. I sighed and gave my head a small shake. "I am nothing. When you see Santa Maria and Drake in hell, explain that to them."

I put two rounds in his head, and he slumped back in his chair. I approached the table and sat. "How about you, Caroline? Are you feeling talkative?"

"Would you shoot me in the head if I wasn't?"

I thought about it for a moment and shook my head. "No, but you are much better off cooperating with me than pissing off the boys who are on their way. They might well take you out to the orchard and shoot you for not cooperating."

"The boys who are coming?"

"Yeah, I called the cavalry."

She smiled. "The cavalry."

"What's so funny? You don't believe me?"

"Do you remember what I asked you when you arrived here with poor Maisy's body, and I asked you to give me a lift to the morgue?"

"Yeah, you asked me if I was some kind of cop."

"Why do you think I asked you that?"

"For the same reason the sheriff did. Because you thought my questions were the same kind of questions a cop would ask."

She was shaking her head. "You were such a brute, and you talked so much shit about being with the CIA when you so obviously weren't, you actually convinced me you were just retired SAS, some kind of soldier of fortune."

"What are you talking about, Caroline?"

"This cavalry that is about to descend on us when the storm dies down. That wouldn't be Brigadier Alexander 'Buddy' Byrd, would it?"

I confess the question caught me by surprise. All I could do was frown and wonder at what point I had stepped through the looking glass. She burst out laughing.

"Who the hell do you think contacted him in the first place? Where do you think his original intelligence came from?"

"You?"

"Have you met anyone else on this island who might be a likely candidate?"

I thought about it. It made perfect sense. All I could say was, "You. When I arrived, you thought the brigadier had sent me. That's why you asked."

"But you were too clever for me. Forgive me, Harry, but I decided to use you. I couldn't do anything. I had contacted the brigadier but seemed to have hit a brick wall. Then you showed up, and I had no choice. I had to do something to put an end to what they were doing. And you proved to be formidable."

I frowned, struggling to understand. "But how do you know about the brigadier?"

"*All* I know about him was what I found on Google, that he had been commander in chief of the British SAS. Britain has some history with the island, so I appealed to him to do something because we were stateless and could not appeal to any international authority. We had slipped through the net. He didn't answer, which is I suppose to be expected. Then you showed up."

I holstered my Sig and rubbed my face with my right hand. My left was still useless. I was in excruciating pain, and my head was spinning.

"So you were never with them."

"Never. I hated the bastards, but as I told you, I am no hero, and I was powerless against them. Harry, you are badly hurt, and I need to patch you up." I nodded. "Come on. Let me get you to my house where I have my medical kit and we are not surrounded by dead bodies."

I nodded again. "Yeah, OK, let's go."

NINETEEN

She drove in silence, and I sat with my eyes closed until we pulled into her drive. Then she punched me gently on the arm.

"C'mon, big guy. Let's get you fixed up."

I climbed out of the old Toyota, and every step that brought me closer to the house was a cacophony of pain in my whole body. My left arm was throbbing, and my eyes and brain were aching for sleep. I felt her reach around me, and she pulled my arm across her shoulders.

"You can come in the front door this time," she said, and there was a smile in her voice.

She unlocked the door, and in her living room, she set me down in an armchair and switched on the lamps she had on low tables by the sofa and the chairs. They cast shadows into the corners, and a moment later she was kneeling, taking off my boots.

"Boy," I heard her mutter, "You are one tough son of a bitch."

Then she was tugging gently, getting me to lean forward.

"Come on, let me get your shirt and your jeans off before you go to sleep. I need to clean these wounds fast or you're going to get complications."

She peeled my clothes off, laid some towels on the sofa, and made me lie on them. After that I drifted in and out of darkness. I dreamed of the film *The 13th Warrior*. The Vikings in their drakkar moving through the silent mist. Occasionally there is the hiss of a flaming arrow as it hurtles into the unseen.

Hot water on my arm brought me back. "This is going to hurt." There was the cold touch of rubbing alcohol followed by the excruciating burn as it bit into the wound. Then the cool soothing of cream.

"This is a topical antibiotic. I'm going to give you some tablets too. It doesn't look infected, but let's play it safe. We can't see what's in there."

I closed my eyes again. Play it safe. The brigadier telling me, "Never get into a fight you can't win." Play it safe. We can't see what's in there. In that group of Norsemen, there was an Islamic ambassador, and he was writing in the sand, *There is but one God and Mohammed is his prophet.*

I sat up with a start. The pain was less. Outside the window, I could see the limpid light of the streetlamps on the empty road. Beyond them was the vast, black ocean. I looked around the room. The lamps cast shadows under their dim, amber glow. The doc was not there.

I looked down at my naked body, my arms and legs. There were Band-Aids, and where the wounds were deeper, she had used bandages. I felt cold and shuddered, and then I heard a door close. Somehow I knew it was the back door, the kitchen door.

Her silhouette appeared at the far end of the room, where a

passage led to the kitchen. She stood motionless and dark, watching me. Her voice seemed disembodied when she spoke.

"You're awake."

"My dream woke me. I was cold."

"I took out the trash."

She came closer, and as she bent to put her cell on the coffee table, the light from the lamp touched her face. She smiled and hunkered down beside me. She touched my forehead, then stroked my face.

"No fever. You are one tough customer." Her smile became rueful. "In another life, in another world... I'll get you something to keep you warm. Lie down." She stood but stayed looking down at me. Then she reached out her hand. "Better still, let's get you into bed."

She led me into her bedroom. The lights were off, but streetlight filtered through the window. She turned down the bed and whispered, "Lie down" and started to undress.

I didn't lie down. I sat and watched her take her clothes off. As she reached behind her back to unfasten her bra, I said, "You're not an islander."

She froze with her bra hanging from her fingers. After a moment, she dropped it to the floor.

"What are you talking about?"

"Your accent. Your accent is English. Your features. I thought you were descended from African slaves and native Indians, but that was an assumption."

There was a frown in her voice. "What are you getting at, Harry? Are you racist?"

"No. You are Afro-Iranian, right? From southern Iran, Hormozgan? Sistan? Maybe Balochistan?" She didn't answer. We remained staring at each other in the half light. "Your parents, maybe your grandparents, went to the UK as refugees after the coup in '79? Maybe they didn't support the Ayatollah's brand of Islam. Maybe they were too Persian and not Iranian enough. But as you grew up in the UK of the twenty-first century, you absorbed the Islamic propaganda that is so prevalent in that country now. Like an Iranian mullah told me once, there is no such thing as fundamentalist Islam or radical Islam. There is only Islam, subjugation to Allah and his prophet, Mohammed. You cannot interpret the word of God. His word is absolute."

She hunkered down in front of me, peering into my face, with the dim, amber light from the street outside touching her beautiful skin.

"Harry, honey, maybe you have got a touch of fever. You have been through hell, but you need to cool down and relax. Yes, I am English, but I am not an Iranian, Muslim fundamentalist. Take it easy, will you?" She smiled and stroked my face. "Come on, lie down and let me cuddle up and make you feel better."

She stood and made to walk around the other side of the bed.

"That's why you contacted the brigadier." She stopped dead. "Why contact the ex-commander of the SAS? Why not contact the current commander? He would be easier to locate, and in the very unlikely event that he decided to do something, he would be in a better position to do so."

"Boy." She said it to the floor. "You're really going to do this, aren't you?"

"Are you going to answer the question? How did you know the brigadier would be in a position to do something?"

"I didn't. It was an act of desperation. Maybe God guided my hand. I got lucky. I told you I didn't even realize you were his man. I mean, why would I..."

She trailed off and sighed. She walked around to the other side of the bed and climbed in. I waited a beat until I heard her move and lie down. Then I stood and turned. She was lying, watching me with her hand under the pillow.

"Is that a long, thin blade, Doc?" She didn't move. She didn't speak. "The akolouthos were brutes, monsters, savage and violent. Hell, they ate their victims alive. But there wasn't a single bite mark on any of the girls, was there? They were punched and beaten first, by a man with big hands. That could have been Santa Maria or da Silva. What was it, some kind of sexual ritual at the Temple? And when they were done, what did you do? You moved in and surgically murdered the girls."

Now she said quietly, "Why would I do a thing like that?"

"It was part of your cover. You had to be a part of the cabal, to find out what they were doing, how close they were to developing their weapons, weapons that would seriously shift the balance of power in the US's favor and weaken Russia and Iran's jihad. Above all, you needed to know if Israel would benefit from this research."

"Come and lie down with me, baby. You're delirious. What you are saying makes no sense. You know it doesn't."

I walked around the bed and stood in front of her. "Kill me," I said, and I was aware that on some level I meant it. She looked infinitely sad and swung her legs out of bed like she was going to hug me and kiss me. I knew what was coming. In the last second, her face twisted with hatred and rage, and she lunged at me with a long, cold steel blade in her hand.

I am not an innocent, fifteen year-old girl. I am the angel of vengeance, *Mal'akh ha-Neqamah*, and I am the meanest son of a bitch in the Valley of Death. Before she got close, I put a right hook through her jaw that sent her crashing against the bedframe before bouncing off and collapsing onto the bedside table, where she dragged the lamp to the floor. I picked up the knife and dropped it on the bed.

I paused. The rain had eased. Away in the distance, I could hear the throb of approaching choppers.

I found her boots, pulled out the laces, and used them to tie her ankles. Then I tied her wrists behind her back. Then I picked her up and dumped her on the bed and wrapped her in a sheet, just in case she had some vestige of modesty to protect.

I walked into the living room and pulled on my jeans and my shirt, then found the bottle of Bells and poured myself a stiff shot. I stood sipping it, looking out of the window at the darkest hour before the dawn. Dotted here and there against the blackness, I could see the spots of the choppers as they approached across the sea.

Don't miss BAD BLOOD. The riveting sequel in the Harry Bauer Thriller series.

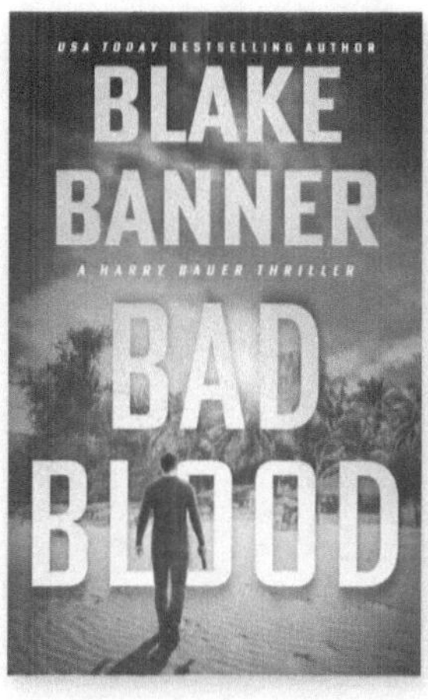

Scan the QR code below to purchase
BAD BLOOD.

Or go to: righthouse.com/bad-blood

NOTE: flip to the very end to read an exclusive sneak peek...

WANT MORE FROM THIS WORLD?

Right House readers get access to **exclusive origin stories**—full-length prequels written only for this list and unavailable anywhere else.

Start with the Harry Bauer origin story, *MARKED FOR DEATH*, by visiting:

vip.righthouse.com/harry-bauer

Or scan the QR code to get instant access.

(Easy to unsubscribe. No spam. Ever.)

ALSO BY BLAKE BANNER

Up to date books can be found at:
www.righthouse.com/blake-banner

ROGUE THRILLERS

Gates of Hell (Book 1)
Hell's Fury (Book 2)
Ice Burn (Book 3)
Judgement by Fire (Book 4)

ALEX MASON THRILLERS

Odin (Book 1)
Ice Cold Spy (Book 2)
Mason's Law (Book 3)
Assets and Liabilities (Book 4)
Russian Roulette (Book 5)
Executive Order (Book 6)
Dead Man Talking (Book 7)
All The King's Men (Book 8)
Flashpoint (Book 9)
Brotherhood of the Goat (Book 10)
Dead Hot (Book 11)
Blood on Megiddo (Book 12)
Son of Hell (Book 13)
Merchant of Death (Book 14)
Extinction C-14 (Book 15)
A Vengeful God (Book 16)
First Blood (Book 17)

HARRY BAUER THRILLER SERIES

Dead of Night (Book 1)
Dying Breath (Book 2)
The Einstaat Brief (Book 3)
Quantum Kill (Book 4)
Immortal Hate (Book 5)
The Silent Blade (Book 6)
LA: Wild Justice (Book 7)
Breath of Hell (Book 8)
Invisible Evil (Book 9)
The Shadow of Ukupacha (Book 10)
Sweet Razor Cut (Book 11)
Blood of the Innocent (Book 12)
Blood on Balthazar (Book 13)
Simple Kill (Book 14)
Riding The Devil (Book 15)
The Unavenged (Book 16)
The Devil's Vengeance (Book 17)
Bloody Retribution (Book 18)
Rogue Kill (Book 19)
Blood for Blood (Book 20)
The Cell (Book 21)
Time to Die (Book 22)
The Reaper of Zion (Book 23)
Justice Without Mercy (Book 24)
Bad Blood (Book 25)

DEAD COLD MYSTERY SERIES

An Ace and a Pair (Book 1)
Two Bare Arms (Book 2)
Garden of the Damned (Book 3)
Let Us Prey (Book 4)

The Sins of the Father (Book 5)
Strange and Sinister Path (Book 6)
The Heart to Kill (Book 7)
Unnatural Murder (Book 8)
Fire from Heaven (Book 9)
To Kill Upon A Kiss (Book 10)
Murder Most Scottish (Book 11)
The Butcher of Whitechapel (Book 12)
Little Dead Riding Hood (Book 13)
Trick or Treat (Book 14)
Blood Into Wine (Book 15)
Jack In The Box (Book 16)
The Fall Moon (Book 17)
Blood In Babylon (Book 18)
Death In Dexter (Book 19)
Mustang Sally (Book 20)
A Christmas Killing (Book 21)
Mommy's Little Killer (Book 22)
Bleed Out (Book 23)
Dead and Buried (Book 24)
In Hot Blood (Book 25)
Fallen Angels (Book 26)
Knife Edge (Book 27)
Along Came A Spider (Book 28)
Cold Blood (Book 29)
Curtain Call (Book 30)

THE OMEGA SERIES

Dawn of the Hunter (Book 1)
Double Edged Blade (Book 2)
The Storm (Book 3)
The Hand of War (Book 4)

A Harvest of Blood (Book 5)
To Rule in Hell (Book 6)
Kill: One (Book 7)
Powder Burn (Book 8)
Kill: Two (Book 9)
Unleashed (Book 10)
The Omicron Kill (Book 11)
9mm Justice (Book 12)
Kill: Four (Book 13)
Death In Freedom (Book 14)
Endgame (Book 15)

ABOUT US

Right House is an independent publisher created by authors for readers. We specialize in Action, Thriller, Mystery, and Crime novels.

If you enjoyed this novel, then there is a good chance you will like what else we have to offer! Please stay up to date by using any of the links below.

Join our mailing lists to stay up to date -->
righthouse.com/email
Visit our website --> righthouse.com
Contact us --> contact@righthouse.com

 facebook.com/righthousebooks
 x.com/righthousebooks
 instagram.com/righthousebooks

EXCLUSIVE SNEAK PEEK OF...

BAD BLOOD

CHAPTER 1

I WAS ON VICTORIA ISLAND, TWO HUNDRED MILES off the coast of Mauritania, trying to escape from my ghosts. The brigadier had told me he'd spent a couple of weeks there a few years back, and it was an earthly paradise. Standing on the boulevard by the port, looking at the sun sparkling off the transparent, turquoise ocean beyond the yachts, I was beginning to feel he might be right. The three girls chatting and laughing beside a row of palm trees and the pretty ketch that was moored there did nothing to diminish that feeling. There was a freshness and an innocence to their beauty that went beyond their lustrous, blue-black hair, their deep brown eyes, and their even tans. It even went beyond their shy smiles as I walked past.

I returned their smiles, reminded myself that one of the reasons I had escaped from New York to Victoria Island was to escape from relationships that were becoming excessively complicated, and kept walking toward the Café del Puerto on the far side of the road. As I walked, the brigadier came to my mind again—him and Colonel Jane Harris. I had been strongly drawn to the colonel at one time. Now I wondered if either of them realized how they felt about each other.

I arrived at the terraced café, chose a table in the sun, and sat. I could still see the three girls. Two of them had sat on a low wall that separated the boulevard from the marina. The one who was standing had cutoff jeans and a mauve T-shirt. It struck me how young they seemed in the playful way they were giggling and talking to each other. I figured they were in their late teens, maybe early twenties. It seemed like yesterday, though my teens had not been playful or innocent. I had spent them learning efficient ways to kill with the British Special Air Service: the SAS.

The waiter came, and I ordered a beer. As he went to get it, I noticed a convertible silver Merc Cabrio roll up across the road. Two guys got out and started talking to the girls. Something made me keep watching. The girls didn't look too enthusiastic, despite the fancy soft-top, and my instinct told me the guys were coming on a bit too strong. Sometimes a Galahad complex can get you in trouble when you go shoving your nose into other people's business. But when I saw one of the guys grab the girl with the denim shorts and start pulling her toward the Merc, I got to my feet.

She pulled free, and her friends grabbed hold of her, pulling her back. The guys were laughing. I hesitated. I told myself if they got back in the car and left, I'd sit and have my beer. They didn't. They closed in on the girls, and their body language got heavy. The waiter came out with my beer. I told him, "Call the cops," and I crossed the road at a trot. Halfway across, I heard the squeal of brakes and an accelerating engine. I glanced to my left and saw a dark Audi sedan approaching fast from the downtown area. I reached the far side, about thirty or forty yards from where the three girls and the two guys had broken into a struggle.

I shouted, "*Hey!*" but my voice was drowned out by the accelerating engine.

I looked back and saw the car approaching fast and that the nearside rear window was open. My reaction was instinctive. I broke into a sprint, bellowing at the top of my voice, "*Get down! Get down!*"

I reached for my Sig. It wasn't there. They were twenty yards away. I was closing. The girls were shouting at the two guys. One drew back his hand to strike out. Then they all must have heard it. They stopped, turned, and stared. The Audi crossed the central greenway. I bellowed, "*For Christ's sake! Get down! Get down!*"

Then everything played out in slow motion. The girl in the cut-off jeans shifted her gaze to stare at me. She was frowning. She had no idea. She didn't understand about killing and murder or what I was doing there. I saw her face in microscopic detail. I saw her long black hair. I saw a wisp trail across her brow. I saw the small crease between her eyebrows as she frowned.

I heard the Audi overtaking me. Every muscle in my back and legs screamed and strained as I ran. My heart thundered. I knew what was going to happen. I knew it mustn't happen. I screamed till my throat and lungs were raw. "*Get down! Get down! Get down!*"

But it was too late. The rattle and crackle started as the brakes screeched. The car lurched and slowed as it turned into a sharp U. It must have been little more than three or four seconds at most while the two automatic rifles rained fire on the group. The boys ran for the Merc but were cut down after only a couple of strides. The two girls who'd been sitting on the wall fell to the ground, covering their heads with their arms. The girl in the shorts stood paralyzed, her eyes locked on mine as I ran. I heard the last six shots clatter out above the squeal of the brakes. I saw the first kick a fountain of concrete from the sidewalk. The second and third hit the wall, and I heard them whine as they ricocheted into space. The fourth hit her belly, and I saw her wince and lean forward. The fifth and sixth hit her in the chest. Her eyes glazed, and her legs folded.

I reached her and fell on my knees beside her as the Audi screamed away into the town. I took her hand and stared into her fading eyes. I wanted to tell her she was going to be all right, that the ambulance was coming, but a grotesque, monstrous pool of blood was spreading underneath her. Her beautiful face, so full of life just moments before, turned waxy. Her eyes held mine, like she wondered if I was going to help her, and then she was gone. She simply ceased to exist.

Far off, a siren wailed across the afternoon. Soon others joined it, growing louder. I heard movement behind me. I looked and saw the two girls who had been with her hunkered down beside me. One of them, in jeans and a pink blouse, stared at me in horror, scrambled to her feet, and ran. The other, younger, in a red dress, just stared at the dead girl. There was a strange mixture of horror and disbelief on her face.

"I tried to warn you," I said, and my voice sounded strange in my own ears.

Her eyes, huge, shifted to mine, like she couldn't understand what I was saying.

"Who are you?"

My answer came like I was drunk. "Harry," I said. "I'm

Harry." Then I looked down at the dead girl. My voice was barely a whisper. "Who is she?"

"She's Miriam." The street seemed to rock. "She was Miriam."

Next thing she was up on her feet and running away, the way her friend had run. As I watched her disappearing form, behind me, I became aware of the howling of the sirens, the screeching of tires on blacktop, and the slamming of doors. Then there were running feet and the crackle of radios and voices.

"*Let me see your hands. Get to your feet nice and slow.*"

I saw her red dress diminishing, vanishing among the people walking on the boulevard. It must have been no more than a second, but the moment was timeless.

Miriam.

Miriam, back in Al-Landy. Her dark eyes staring at me, asking for help.

I turned back. There were two guys in uniform pointing guns at me. Between them was a third guy. He was small and skinny in chinos and a jacket that was too big for him. His hair was tight and curly, and he had a nose like a sharp hook and long, dark eyes. He had a pistol in his right hand but wasn't pointing it at me.

I shifted my gaze to the girl's dead eyes. I let go of her hand and stood, showing the cops my empty palms. The guy I figured was the detective waved me away from the body.

"Come over here. Let the boys do their work." To the cops he said, "We're OK here. Go seal the area."

I walked where he was gesturing. He put his hand on my arm and guided me a little farther away, to the palm tree where the girls had been standing. He jerked his chin at me. "You OK?"

"Yeah, I'm OK."

"What's your name?"

"My name's Harry Bauer." I pointed at the two boys lying twisted in spreading pools of blood. There were men in hazmat suits bending over them. "They were getting rough with the girls."

His eyes narrowed. "You shot them?" He sounded incredulous.

"No. It was three men in an Audi sedan."

He gave a single, upward nod. "What girls?"

"There were three girls. Two of them survived and ran when you arrived. One, slim, five-seven, maybe seventeen or eighteen years old, long black hair, loose, a red dress. The other, similar size and build, black hair in a ponytail, jeans and a pink shirt. They headed west along the boulevard."

He called over a uniform and told him to put out a BOLO for the girls. The cop ran to his car. The detective pulled out his wallet and showed me his badge.

"Detective Ismael Martinez. Homicide. You know those boys?" He jerked his head at the corpses.

"No. I'm from New York. I've never been here before." I arched an eyebrow at him. "I'm on vacation. They told me this was a paradise on Earth."

He snorted something that might have been a laugh in another lifetime. "Well," he said. "It's on Earth. They got that part right. You say they were getting rough?"

"I was on my way to the café." I pointed across the road where I could see my beer on the table and the waiter watching. "The girls were standing right here, by this tree." I took a breath, wondering why this had affected me. It was just another killing among the hundreds I had witnessed. "We smiled at each other. I got to the bar and ordered a beer. That one." I pointed at it sitting on the table. "Then those boys pulled up in that convertible Merc." I pointed at it. "They started coming on to the girls. They started getting rough, and I started to come over and tell the guys to move on..." I trailed off and shrugged. "As I crossed the road, the Audi showed up."

I told him the rest of the story. He made notes. Without looking up, he asked, "Did you get the plates?"

I shook my head. "No. I was looking at Miriam, shouting at her to get down."

"Miriam." It wasn't a question. "You knew her name."

"Her friend, in the red dress, told me her name was Miriam."

"I'm going to need you to sign a statement at the police station on St. John's Avenue."

I nodded, looking at the two bodies that were now being lifted onto gurneys and wheeled toward the meat wagons.

"That was a pretty reckless drive-by. Either they didn't care if they were caught, or they were confident they wouldn't be." I turned to look into his face. "You asked me if I knew them. Are they gang members? Is this a vendetta? A gang war?"

He sighed and fished a pack of Marlboro from his pocket. He poked one in his mouth and lit up with a blue, disposable lighter which he held in his fist. He inhaled deeply and let the smoke out as he spoke.

"Your friend was right. This used to be a small paradise. Then Trump started building his wall and sinking yachts off Venezuela." He studied my face a moment. "We're not talking about some half-assed criminal organization. We're talking about one of the biggest, most profitable industries on the planet. Am I wrong?"

I shook my head. "You're not wrong."

He wagged a long, brown finger at me. "And an industry

run by the most cruel, ruthless bastards on the planet. So when Trump closes those two doors to them, what are they going to do? Go home crying to their mommies?"

"It's a story I've heard before," I told him. "They are looking for alternative routes into Europe and the USA."

He nodded. "The islands in the Atlantic. Islands with ties to the old empires. The Azores for access to Portugal, the Canaries for access to Spain. Victoria Island with access—" He raised his right hand holding up four fingers with his cigarette stuck between two of them. "The United Kingdom, Gibraltar, North Africa and the Middle East. Suddenly our paradise is overrun with South American drug dealers and—"

"And Middle Eastern arms dealers."

He nodded slowly and looked at his cigarette as he flicked ash. "You know something about this."

"I was in the British SAS for a few years. They used to send us out on loan for operations in Mexico and Colombia, and Afghanistan."

He let a smile ride up the side of his face, still looking at the ember on the end of his cigarette. "I wish they would send you on loan to Victoria Island, Mr. Bauer. Our little paradise is becoming hell." He pointed with his chin at the departing ambulance. "These kids, the worst thing they would do a couple of years ago is pick a pocket, snatch a bag, or get into a fight at a nightclub. Now they're hyped up on coke, with a hundred thousand dollars stuffed in shoe boxes under their beds, and they think they are indestructible, protected by the great drug lords..."

He trailed off. I watched him a moment.

"And are they?"

He gave a snort. He still wouldn't meet my eye.

"You know why Lucifer got kicked out of heaven and

wound up in hell? Because Jehovah had more guns and wasn't afraid to use them. The problem with paradise, Mr. Bauer, is that the people who live there get soft. And when they are confronted with demons who are accustomed to blood and real, uninhibited violence, they become terrified and are liable to cave in."

He dropped his cigarette on the sidewalk and crushed it with his foot.

"Drop by the police station tomorrow midmorning to sign your statement, if you will, Mr. Bauer. Thank you for your help today. I am sorry about your vacation. It didn't use to be like this."

He moved to walk away, but I stopped him.

"Who's the girl, Miriam?"

He looked down at his shoes. "Why?"

"She seemed like a nice kid. They all looked similar. I got the feeling they were sisters. They must have parents. This is going to be traumatic for them. I figure they'd like to know what happened firsthand."

He spoke with a smile but no malice. "A real live Sir Galahad, huh?" He came back a couple of steps. "Eva, Miriam, and Carmen Scott. This is a small town on a small island. Most people know each other. Miriam's mother is Mary. Her husband was an island man, but his great-grandfather was an English settler. He was the governor, in fact, back when this was a British territory. Humphrey, that's Miriam's father, was the mayor of this town for many years. We all liked and respected him. I knew him personally. He was a good man."

"You're talking in the past tense."

"He was shot and killed two years back, outside City Hall."

"But you never caught who did it."

"I don't need to spell it out, right?" He sighed. "She'd

appreciate your visit, I'm sure. She has an apartment on Red Lion Avenue. I'll tell her you're coming. I'll give you a call when I'm done."

"I appreciate it."

He gave a single nod, and I watched him walk away.

CHAPTER 2

I LEFT MY BEER TO GET WARM IN THE CAFÉ AND walked along Queen Victoria Boulevard toward Imperial Circus. There was a gentle sun that reflected in small, liquid flashes off the dark water. A salty breeze touched my skin and moved the awnings over the street cafés. There was a row of five fishing boats drawn up on the sand, where two old guys sat smoking, fixing their nets. For a moment, it struck me that there was a rough beauty to the scene: a beauty that was born of sanity.

The word made me stop and look more closely at the blue and white wooden boats, at the white sand and the dark blue ocean, and the old guys with their cigarette butts hanging from the corners of their mouths as they stitched their nets.

Sanity.

This island had been a paradise of sanity, and now these bastards had brought their madness, their sickness to these people's lives. I remembered Detective Ismael Martinez's words: "The problem with paradise, Mr. Bauer, is that the people who live there get soft. When they are confronted with demons who are accustomed to blood and violence, they are liable to cave in."

Maybe, I thought, as I turned and walked on toward the Imperial Hotel, that was why nature created men like me, so that our sickness might give sanity a fighting chance. The thought didn't make me smile. There was a sour bitterness in me as I played over in my mind Miriam's last seconds as she held my hand.

A fighting chance? She'd had no fighting chance. She'd been hanging out with her sisters, laughing, playing, and the jackals and the hyenas had closed in, with nothing but rape and murder on their minds. My existence had given her no fighting chance. Just as in Al-Landy, in the deserts of Afghanistan, my existence had given that other Miriam no fighting chance. Bitterness twisted like a snake inside me. This island hadn't become hell. The whole damned planet had become hell.

The Imperial Hotel stood on the Imperial Circus, overlooking the Atlantic Ocean, just a hundred yards from the sea. It was, as the name suggested, a leftover from the days of the British Empire. It was a large, solid colonial building with broad windows and an elegant mahogany and brass entrance under a magnificent Palladian portico. Inside, the foyer was hushed, and the staff wore black trousers and white wing-collars under burgundy jackets. By the look of them, I suspected they were the original staff from 1859, when the hotel first opened.

It was perfect. It was also up for sale, and no doubt it would be replaced by some kind of concrete and glass monstrosity aimed at drawing in cheap tourism to further kill any resemblance to paradise.

I made my way to the dining room, which had crystal chandeliers suspended from a high, stucco ceiling and lots of elaborate gold leaf. I had a couple of martinis and forced myself to eat a sirloin steak. My phone didn't ring or ping, and after a coffee and a Bushmills, I went up to my room to retrieve my Sig Sauer P226 from the insulated compartment in my suitcase.

After that, I stretched out on my bed, staring at the shadows under the ceiling. They were the same shadows that hung out under my ceiling in New York. I'd obviously brought them with me. That was no surprise. I took them with me wherever I went. I asked them for the millionth time what the point was: What was the point of Miriam's death in Afghanistan? What was the point of Miriam's death here on Victoria Island? What was the point of all the pointless rapes and murders that had become routine and banal, a part of daily life on this godforsaken planet? What was the point of any of it?

They gave me the same answer they always gave me. They ignored me. Which made me wonder, just before I drifted into a troubled sleep, what was the point of asking them?

I DIDN'T HEAR from Detective Ismael Martinez until the following morning at breakfast.

"Detective, good morning."

"I spoke to Mary yesterday. She was in a bad way, as you can imagine. She said she would see you this morning, about ten o'clock. When you're done with her, you could pass by the station. It's like five hundred yards. Down Red Lion, take a left on Fennel Street, and the station is on the corner with St. John. Ask for me at the desk."

I told him I would, hung up, and poured myself another cup of coffee from the silver coffee pot into the bone china cup.

I managed a wry smile. No wonder the brigadier thought it was paradise. He and the hotel both belonged in the 19th century.

It was a short walk along Red Lion Avenue from the Imperial Hotel to Mary Scott's apartment. Hers was the top floor of a six-story block built back in the 1930s. It had cute Art Deco touches on the main entrance and on the broad, bow windows that ran down the center of the top five stories. In the lobby, the light was dim, and the small brass lamps on the walls, with their ancient red shades trimmed with gold, did little to dispel the gloom. On the left, there was a highly polished mahogany desk. Behind it, a door stood open onto a small room, where I could see a kettle and a carton of milk. Sitting behind the desk with a steaming mug was a guy who was probably already old when they built the block. He had a fishing magazine open in front of him, but he was looking at me with a face that said he just knew I was going to spoil his break by making him talk. I nodded and smiled and made my way to the elevator I could see across the lobby.

It was one of those concertina affairs and was probably cutting-edge technology when they installed it. The buttons were in the British style, where the ground floor is G and the second floor is 1. Following that British logic, I pressed 5, and it took me to the sixth floor. Absently, as the ancient machine cranked me to the top of the building, I wondered if that somehow explained how one of the smallest countries on the planet managed to have the biggest empire in history. They pressed five and got to six. When the car juddered to a halt, I dismissed the thought, fought the concertina open, and made my way along a broad passage carpeted in sage green, with more of those cute brass lamps with red and gold shades stuck to the walls.

The door was opened by a woman in a maid's uniform

with a bonnet and an apron. I told her, “Mrs. Scott? I am Harry Bauer.”

She said, “Pliss” and gestured me into a large entrance hall with a small dresser and a vast mirror. On the left, there were heavy wooden doors with glass panels, each displaying an Art Deco flower. She knocked and stepped in. After a moment, she stepped out again and held the door open for me.

It wasn’t anything you could call a living room. The brigadier would have insisted it was very much a drawing room. There were glass-paneled doors that folded back onto a large balcony festooned with ferns and flowers set around cane furniture. In front of that, there was a handsome Steinway mini grand piano. The wall behind it was lined with low bookcases. On the left, the room opened out into an ample area with a green sofa under the bow window and too many chairs, occasional tables, plants, and photographs. It was fussy but lived in and comfortable.

Standing at the sofa was a woman in her sixties. At five-seven, she gave the impression of being taller. Her hair was jet black and pulled back into a bun. She was dressed in a black velvet dress, and her eyes, which were large and dark, were swollen from crying but sharp and intelligent. Her English was perfect, with just a hint of an accent.

“Mr. Bauer, won’t you come in? Can I offer you some coffee or tea?”

“Mrs. Scott, no, thank you. I won’t keep you. Thank you for seeing me.”

She gave a small nod past my shoulder, and I heard the door close. She sat on the sofa and gestured me to a chair beside a large, ornate lamp. I searched my mind for how to approach what I had to tell her, but she made it easy.

“You saw Miriam just before she was shot.”

I studied her face for a second. The pain was there, plain to see, but so was the strength. She was not a woman who was going to hide from reality.

"Yes. I was taking a morning walk, and I passed Miriam, Eva, and Carmen on the boulevard."

"You noticed them."

I glanced at her. She gave a small smile. I returned it.

"They seemed very happy, talking and laughing with each other."

"They..." She faltered a moment. "Eva and Carmen told me they noticed you."

"We exchanged a smile." I paused. "How old was she, Mary?"

"Just eighteen, last May." She gave a short, wet laugh. "A little Taurus bull. So obstinate with such a temperament! So loyal, protective. Such a good daughter." She looked down at her hands in her lap. Her lip curled, and she shook her head. "She believed in all those things. Astrology, angels, candles... and now look."

We were quiet for a moment. I took a deep breath. "I had just ordered a beer at the café across the road when two boys arrived in a Mercedes convertible. They got out and started talking to Miriam. They tried to make her get in the car with them. Her sisters tried to stop them, and a struggle broke out." She nodded at her hands. I pressed her. "Do you know who those boys were?"

"Ismael told me. Julian Garcia and his brother Elias. Island boys from a wretched family of half-gypsies. I think the mother is Moroccan. Bad people."

"They were the intended victims. A car drove up. There were three men. Two were shooting from the open windows. I didn't get a good look at them, but it was clear Julian and Elias were their intended targets."

She seemed not to hear. "You tried to save Miriam." She raised her eyes to look at me. "Eva and Carmen told me. You came running."

I sighed. "I tried. I saw Julian and Elias struggling with her, pulling her toward their convertible. I was going to..." I hesitated a moment, aware of the woman's class and elegance, and how inappropriate my language would have been. I smiled. "I was going to tell them to leave her alone." My smile faded as I remembered. "When I was crossing the road, the car showed up. I wish I had gone a little sooner."

"She was holding your hand when she died."

I nodded. For a moment, I couldn't speak, but eventually I said, "Yes."

Her voice was barely a whisper. "She was with a friend."

"Do you know who was in that car, Mary?"

She nodded. "I know. It was the same men who killed my husband two years ago. They are not from the island. They are from Mauritania, white Moors from the Bidh'an, Berbers and Arab, Hassaniya-speaking tribes. *Desgraciados!*"

She spat the Spanish word out, closed her eyes, and turned her head.

I frowned. "Mauritanians?"

"They never used to come here. My husband was very active in keeping them out. He knew what they were like. It is a very poor country, Mr. Bauer, because the people are too lazy to exploit their natural resources. They have iron, they have gold, but mining is hard work, so they became a key point on the Sahel route."

I spoke half to myself. "From the Red Sea to the Atlantic

Ocean, through Eritrea and Sudan, Chad, Niger and Mali, to Senegal and Mauritania."

Her eyes narrowed at me. "You know?"

"I've heard something."

"Opium and products extracted from opium come from Myanmar and Afghanistan, along the Sahel route, to enter Europe through Spain and Portugal. But it is not just drugs, Mr. Bauer." She shook her head. "Mauritania also sells slaves. There are many slaves in Mauritania. The white Moors use the black Moors, the Haratin, as slaves. Their women are beautiful. So they sell them in Poland for distribution in Europe and the Middle East, as prostitutes. My husband knew all about this, and he did everything in his power to stop them using our island."

"That's why they killed him."

"Yes. When Trump started sinking the boats coming from Venezuela, they had to find new ways way into the USA and Europe, for drugs and slaves."

"And that was Victoria Island."

"Canary Islands, Spain, and Portugal have started to crack down also, making it more difficult to traffic into Europe from Morocco. So they come to Victoria from Ruheiba Cove. It is three hundred miles. Nobody stops them." She searched my face with her eyes, as though trying to find an answer there. "We have always been peaceful and self-sufficient. The quality of life was always good here. There was no crime and almost zero emigration. The people who lived here wanted to stay here. So we have good historic relations with Portugal and Spain, France, and the United Kingdom. We are not part of Europe, but it is easy for us to get in. We do not need a visa." She sighed and spread her hands. "So now we have Mexicans and Mauritanians, fighting to control the island. Banda S are the Mexicans. They are a gang with many island boys who have joined. The Mauritanians call themselves AQIM."

"Al-Qaeda Islamic Maghreb?"

"Yes."

"Son of a bitch..." I said it to myself, and she arched an eyebrow at me. For just a moment, I felt like I was four years old and said, "Excuse me."

"It is a cancer, Mr. Bauer. It is spreading across the globe like a black shadow, consuming everything in its path. It feeds the darkest parts of the human soul and extinguishes the light." She held my eye for a moment. Then, "You are not a normal man. Your interest in this..." She trailed off and started again. "Are you police? MI6?"

My smile told her she wasn't exactly wrong, but I said, "No, nothing like that."

"A soldier, then."

"I was a soldier."

"Mr. Bauer, I would pay money. I am not rich, but I am not poor. I would pay money for a real man to kill these people and make the gangs leave our island."

My sigh was deeper and more heartfelt than I had intended. "I had better go. I am so sorry I wasn't able to save Miriam."

I was about to stand, but she reached out and took my hand.

"Good people hate violence, Mr. Bauer. We all know that. But my husband knew, I know, and if you were a soldier, you know, that in a world where there is pain, where pain exists, the man who controls violence is king. Peace lovers and gentle, kind people too easily become victims. They are too easy to break and control. Paradise becomes a hunting ground for the devil." She closed her eyes and gave her head a shake. "If we want to live in paradise, we must become masters of violence in order to protect it. That is reality. We cannot escape reality, Mr. Bauer. I beg of you, I will pay if I have to: kill these people. I believe God has sent you to save this island and avenge my daughter. The leader of Banda S is Charlie Mendez. The men from AQIM who killed my husband are Abdallah Ba and Franqui Gallot."

I gave her hand a squeeze and stood. "Thank you for talking to me, Mary."

By the time I got to the door, my belly was on fire. I stopped and looked back. I gave a small shake of my head.

"You don't need to pay a penny," I said. "When peace returns to the island, when Miriam is avenged, then you can buy me a beer."

CHAPTER 3

I ARRIVED AT THE POLICE STATION SHORTLY BEFORE noon and was shown through to Detective Martinez's office on the second floor. It was odd because all the walls were mainly glass, but there were no windows. He had a large desk you couldn't see because it was covered in paper, and he gestured me to a chair across from him as I was shown in.

"Mr. Bauer." He said it like he was checking a box in his mind. "Please sit down."

I sat, and he cleared a space in front of me and dropped my statement into that space. "Please read it and, if you agree with what it says, please sign it."

I read it through, signed it, and handed it back to him.

"You know who did this. You know who killed Humphrey Scott. You know what's happening with Banda S and AQIM. Why don't you arrest them?"

He leaned back in his chair and sighed with a humorless smile stuck on the side of his face.

"Mary Scott. She got to you, huh?"

"Miriam Scott got to me. Mary Scott gave me some background."

"Sure." He nodded. He shrugged and spread his hands and reminded me for a moment of Christopher Walken. "There *is* the question of *evidence*. How do you prove a guy *belongs* to a gang? They don't *carry* membership cards." He held up a hand. "Yeah, I *know*, the NYPD and Scotland Yard do it every *day*. But their personnel runs into thousands. Mine runs to a dozen uniforms and two detectives. I am out*manned* and out*gunned*."

I was about to answer, but he went on.

"Hey! *Mexico* is outmanned and outgunned. What do you think I can do with twelve guys?" He played out the scene for me: "'Hey, Fanqui, where were you yesterday at one p.m.?' 'I was having a party with Jezebel, Fatima, and Sophia. Abdullah and Amir were there.' They will swear to it in court, and next day my wife and my three children are shot dead on the way to school."

"I can't argue with that. How many AQIM are there?"

He wagged a finger at me. "I got curious. I have an instinct. Something about you. You don't raise your voice, but you observe and you ask relevant questions, and that somehow winds up putting you in control. So I pulled your passport details from Passport Control and made some enquiries. SAS, huh?"

"That was a long time ago."

"What you been doing since?"

"A bit of this and a bit of that. Am I being interrogated?"

"No. I'm just curious. Mrs. Scott offer you money?"

"No, and I wouldn't take it if she did. I'm on vacation."

He did his Christopher Walken shrug again. "How many AQIM *are* there? It *fluctuates*. They come and go from Mauritania, in yachts. As few as five, as many as twenty. Usually about ten or twelve."

"How about Banda S? I'm guessing they don't nip back and forth across the Atlantic every week."

"About the same number. You'd be surprised how often a luxury yacht arrives here from Miami via Venezuela or Mexico, flying the Stars and Stripes."

"So they are competing for the same market in Europe, and this is one of the last gateways open. Can't you ask Europol for help, or the UK, Spain, or Portugal?"

He threw back his head and gave a laugh that was surprisingly big in such a small, scrawny guy.

"That funny, huh?" I asked.

He nodded as his laugh trailed off. "Yeah, it's funny. It's also sad. Nah, those guys..." He shook his head. "You know? If they shut the door—the door is Victoria—the shit wouldn't get in. But they prefer to spend a thousand times more money with a thousand cops running around in circles chasing a million small-time pushers instead of just helping us close the door. Bah!"

He gestured at me, "I'm pretty sure I don't need to tell you this, Mr. Bauer, there are *a lot* of interests involved in the narcotics trade—and in the sex slave trade. Not *everybody* wants that trade to stop. You know what I'm saying? Your government has black budgets that run into trillions of dollars. You think Europe hasn't? You think those budgets come out of taxes and value added tax?" He wagged a finger in the negative. "Nah." He shook his head for more emphasis. "Let's make a big, vote-winning show of closing the big, visible doors and kicking out the narcos, but hey! Let's leave a couple of doors open too. Doors nobody ever heard of, like Victoria Island, so we can cream off ten percent to cover our black budgets."

"That's a pretty bleak view."

"What can I say?" He gave that shrug again. "We live in a world where we have to eat each other in order to survive. It's called reality, and it sucks."

"So Miriam's murder goes unpunished? And your island gets taken over by these bastards?"

He leaned forward. "Mr. Bauer, I am going to do everything in my power to punish her killer and save Victoria. But my power, as a detective on this small island with twelve cops at my disposal, is limited. So 'everything in my power' is not going to be even close to enough. So do me a favor. Thanks for your help, but unless you have solutions instead of criticisms, get off my back."

I read him loud and clear. I nodded and stood. At the door, I turned and asked him, "So, just so I can be sure to stay out of harm's way and not cause you more problems than you and your police force can handle, where should I stay away from in order to avoid running into Banda S and AQIM?"

He pointed at me like he really meant it. "You stay away from Mariners Way in the Barracks District. I am serious. You don't go anywhere near Number 2 on that street. I mean it, Mr. Bauer. And the same goes for the Coca Club on Island Route VI and Sail Street, out by the airport. Just stay away from those places. You understand me?"

"Hey, I'm here on vacation. I'm not here to cause trouble. Take it easy."

I stepped out and closed the door a little more forcefully than strictly necessary and stepped out into the street. I stood a moment with my hands in my pockets, staring up and down the street.

Number 2, Mariners Way, in the Barracks district, and the

Coca Club on Island Route VI and Sail Street, out by the airport.

There were only two reasons I could think of for Detective Martinez giving me that information about Banda S and AQIM. Either he wanted me to do to them what he could not do, or he wanted them to do to me what he could not do. Either way, for him it was a win-win.

I began to walk down the hill toward the hotel. The smell of ozone was rich in the air, and a blue and white awning over a pavement café flapped gently in the breeze. The rich, black smell of coffee joined the ozone. Somebody laughed. It was the small things, I told myself, that made paradise.

That reminded me of one late night on the brigadier's terrace, looking out at the Hudson on its way to the sea. He was telling me I should read John Milton, *Paradise Lost*. He'd surprised me by intoning quietly, "Farewell happy fields where joy forever dwells. Hail horrors, hail infernal world, and thou profoundest Hell receive thy new Possessor. One who brings a mind not to be changed by place or time. The mind is its own place, and in itself can make a Heaven of Hell, and a Hell of Heaven. What matter where, if I be still the same?"

The Imperial's parking lot was an area, part scrubland and part derelict site, at the back of the hotel. I had parked my Wrangler Rubicon rental there, and now I made my way through the shrubs and chunks of old beam and concrete, to clamber behind the wheel. I sat a while drumming a tattoo, then fired up the engine and pulled out onto Imperial Circus and took the third exit onto the boulevard where the day before I had seen Miriam gunned down.

I drove south for half a mile, then turned onto Island Route VI and followed that for a little over a mile. It wasn't long before I saw Sail Street on the far side, and on the corner a big open lot which was mainly rust-red dirt with a rough construction at the back end. There were a couple of trucks and a convertible Merc parked outside. Over the door, there was a wooden sign that read *Club Coca*. Beneath that, in running script, it read *Recuerdos de Sinaloa*: Regards from Sinaloa. Nice.

On one side of the writing, there was a picture of a naked girl who might have been Indian or Haratine. On the other side, there was a coca leaf.

Subtle. About as subtle as a sledgehammer.

I pulled across the road and entered the big, dusty lot to pull up in front of the entrance. I climbed down and stepped onto the deck. There was a guy leaning against the jamb, watching me. He was big, maybe six-four or taller, with big shoulders and pale blue eyes. He had a bottle of beer in his hand and a cigarette in his mouth. He inhaled and spoke quietly as he exhaled.

"This is a private club, and even if it weren't, we're closed."

I gave a single nod. "That's OK. I don't need a drink. And if I did, I wouldn't drink here. I need to talk to Charlie Mendez."

His eyes traveled down to my boots and then up to my face. They were smiling, but he wasn't. A couple of guys came out of the shadows behind him to stand on the deck and look at me.

"You know," he said, "Sometimes I don't express myself so good. What I meant to say was, get the fuck of my deck, off my lot, and out of my face. Go."

"No. You were very clear. I think maybe it was me who didn't make myself clear. I didn't say I needed to talk to a fucking gorilla with the IQ of a piece of cow shit. I said I needed to talk to Charlie Mendez. So how about you do your job and go get him?"

He grinned and spat elaborately on the deck.

"Boy, I am going to hurt you so bad."

The two guys who'd come out to watch started laughing. One of them was young, maybe eighteen. The other was the dangerous one. He was in his late thirties, and what he'd lost in speed and agility, he'd gained in experience.

The big gorilla didn't drop his cigarette or put down his beer. He was going to make an exhibition of me and beat me to a pulp while smoking and drinking. But of course, if his hands were full, he was going to have to use his feet. So as he took his second step, I smashed the heel of my boot into the gap on the inside of his right kneecap, and as my foot touched the floor, I twisted my heel and put a right hook right through his head. He did a brief Elvis impersonation and fell heavily on his back.

By the time the other two had finished processing what had happened, I had the P226 in my hand, and I was pointing it at the gorilla's head.

"I didn't come here to kill anybody. I came here to talk. So how about you boys do this asshole a favor and go and get me Charlie Mendez?"

"I'm right here. What the hell do you want?"

He was standing in the doorway. He was maybe thirty, slim and hard with short, very black hair. He had a Mexican accent and the kind of dead eyes that told you he didn't need to be a sociopath to kill people and not give a damn.

"I want to talk to you about AQIM."

"What's AQIM to you?"

"I know who they are, and I saw what they did to your boys on the boulevard. I figure you want them punished."

He shrugged. "Again, what the fuck's that to you?"

“I’m getting there. They also killed a girl. She was only eighteen, and she happened to be a girl I liked. I want payback. I figure you want payback too.”

“Fuck you. Look around you. You think I need you to kick AQIM’s ass?”

“Yeah, I do. AQIM are backed by Al-Qaeda. It’s what the A-Q stands for. Did you know that? I was in special ops for eight years. I know these people. They are dangerous in ways you can’t imagine.”

He took a step toward me and started doing that weird thing punks do where they bounce on their knees and move their shoulders, like that’s intimidating.

“Yeah? You think I’m scared of a bunch of Ay-rabs? You know what the S stands for in Banda S, asshole?”

“Yeah. You’re going to tell me it stands for Sinaloa. Actually it stands for stupid.” I pointed at him. “All your fights are against guys who are tied to chairs or held by your boys.” I jerked my thumb to the northeast, where I knew AQIM had their HQ. “Those guys are battle-hardened, and they would rather die than submit to an asshole like you or your punks.” I gestured at the gorilla who still lay between me and Mendez and was beginning to groan. “Look at this. This is the kind of tough guy you’re going to send against professional terrorists? You’ll all be dead in a couple of days. Julian and his brother Elias were the first to go down. Believe me, they won’t be the last. They’ll be coming for you within the week. And where they came from”—I pointed east, toward Africa—“there are thousands more.”

I turned and walked toward the Wrangler. Mendez called out after me.

“So what can you do, tough guy? One man?”

“You’ll find out.”

I wrenched open the door, climbed in, and drove away across the dirt.

My idea, if you could call it that, aside from getting a reading on what kind of metal the Banda S was made of, was to try to provoke open warfare between the two gangs. My first impression was that they were not up to much, and what I had told Mendez was probably true. If AQIM really were linked to Al-Qaeda, they would eliminate Banda S without any trouble at all. And the ruthlessness and efficiency I had witnessed the day before seemed to support that.

If that was the case, if I could provoke Banda S into taking out at least some of the opposition, or even persuade them to work with me, that would help. If I couldn't, I'd have to do the job on my own.

I'd faced worse, I told myself, and kind of believed myself. Then, as I followed the VI up into the hills to the east and north of Victoria, I told myself I was about to face worse. Al-Qaeda had been quiet on the international scene for a long time. But of all the Islamic Jihadist groups, they were, and always would be, were the most dangerous. They were smart, adaptable, and well-funded. They had learned from the CIA and the Heritage Program that the best way to fund dark programs is to make your money from the drugs trade.

The illegal narcotics trade not only generates hundreds of billions of dollars every year, it has also generated a vast, intangible network of holding companies and financial networks running from the British Virgin Islands and Panama through the Cayman Islands and Bermuda to Singapore and Hong Kong: a network where dirty money can just disappear and reappear as pristine and white as if you'd washed it with Ariel.

Despite Islam's avowed hatred of narcotics, Al-Qaeda had learned to adapt, and they pretty much controlled the passage of Eastern narcotics from the Red Sea, across Africa to Morocco and Mauritania, where it was then distributed to its markets in Europe and America. The money they made on that passage was then fed into the dark banking system and used for their dark ops. Al-Qaeda was both highly professional and very dangerous.

Scan the QR code below to purchase BAD BLOOD.
Or go to: righthouse.com/bad-blood

www.ingramcontent.com/pod-product-compliance
Lightning Source LLC
LaVergne TN
LVHW091135080826
845145LV00008B/2168

* 9 7 8 1 6 3 6 9 6 4 7 6 8 *